THE FORM OF THINGS UNKNOWN

Also by Robin Bridges

Dreaming of Antigone

Published by Kensington Publishing Corp.

THE FORM OF THINGS UNKNOWN

Robin Bridges

KENSINGTON BOOKS
www.kensingtonbooks.com

To the extent that the image or images on the cover of this book depict a person or persons, such person or persons are merely models, and are not intended to portray any character or characters featured in the book.

This book is a work of fiction. Names, characters, places, and incidents either are products of the author's imagination or are used fictitiously. Any resemblance to actual persons, living or dead, events, or locales is entirely coincidental.

KENSINGTON BOOKS are published by

Kensington Publishing Corp.
119 West 40th Street
New York, NY 10018

Copyright © 2016 by Robin Bridges

All rights reserved. No part of this book may be reproduced in any form or by any means without the prior written consent of the Publisher, excepting brief quotes used in reviews.

All Kensington titles, imprints, and distributed lines are available at special quantity discounts for bulk purchases for sales promotion, premiums, fund-raising, educational, or institutional use.

Special book excerpts or customized printings can also be created to fit specific needs. For details, write or phone the office of the Kensington Sales Manager: Kensington Publishing Corp., 119 West 40th Street, New York, NY 10018. Attn. Sales Department. Phone: 1-800-221-2647.

Kensington and the K logo Reg. U.S. Pat. & TM Off.

eISBN-13: 978-1-4967-0357-6
eISBN-10: 1-4967-0357-X
First Kensington Electronic Edition: September 2016

ISBN-13: 978-1-4967-0356-9
ISBN-10: 1-4967-0356-1
First Kensington Trade Paperback Printing: September 2016

10 9 8 7 6 5 4 3 2 1

Printed in the United States of America

For Parham

Acknowledgments

Most heartfelt thanks to my amazing agent, Ethan, for his never-ending support for this book. To Alicia Condon, my wonderful editor, to Jane Nutter, marketing maven, to the eternally patient Paula Reedy, to Kristine Mills for my gorgeous Kensington covers, and to the rest of the phenomenal people at Kensington, you all have my undying gratitude.

This is probably the most difficult book I've ever written. What began as a typical ghost story grew into something more frightening when I realized the things Natalie thought she saw weren't really there. According to the latest numbers from the National Alliance on Mental Illness, one in five teenagers have or will have a serious mental illness. Which means we're all in this together. Don't be afraid to ask for help. And don't be afraid to ask if someone needs help. Love and thanks to you all from the very bottom of this grateful writer's heart.

The lunatic, the lover and the poet
Are of imagination all compact:
One sees more devils than vast hell can hold,
That is, the madman: the lover, all as frantic,
Sees Helen's beauty in a brow of Egypt:
The poet's eye, in fine frenzy rolling,
Doth glance from heaven to earth, from earth to heaven;
And as imagination bodies forth
The forms of things unknown, the poet's pen
Turns them to shapes and gives to airy nothing
A local habitation and a name.

—Theseus, *A Midsummer Night's Dream,* act 5, scene 1

CHAPTER 1

The course of true love never did run smooth.
—*A Midsummer Night's Dream,* act 1, scene 1

My grandmother is listening to the Beatles again. Loudly. She refuses to use earbuds because she says bugs can crawl out of the tiny speakers and into your brain that way. John Lennon's voice travels up the stairs and under the doors and through the thin walls of this smelly old house. Lennon's lyrics reach me all the way up here in the attic, where my parents have cleared a space for my mattress and a small bookshelf for my sketch pads. Your castle in the sky, my mother joked. I'm the madwoman in the attic, I joked back.

Mom didn't laugh.

Grandma particularly loves "Strawberry Fields." She says the angels talk to her through this song. And I worry that the longer I lie here and listen, I'm going to hear the angels talking to me, too.

My brother doesn't think I'm crazy. At least he doesn't treat me like a crazy person and I'm grateful for that. Ever since I was discharged from Winter Oaks, rated the best adolescent psych unit in eastern Georgia, Mom and Dad have hovered over me, watching me like a ticking time bomb.

They make sure I take my pills, and ask me a million times a day if I'm feeling all right. How should I feel? I'm curled up in my bed under my quilt, even though the attic is hot and stuffy, and I wonder if I can even describe the sensations I'm feeling. I can't call them emotions. At least not right now. There are only a million thoughts. Emotionless thoughts buzzing around in my head like insects.

Thankfully, my parents now have Grandma to worry about. Maybe they'll forget to worry about me. Until I do something terrible. Something crazy.

"Hey, Hippie." David tromps up the stairs and knocks on the door as he's pushing it open.

"What's up, Hick?" I don't bother to raise my head from the pillow.

He plops himself down next to me. Grandma's ancient calico cat has been cuddled up against me all morning. Now she hisses at David and jumps down. "Nat, I need a favor."

"From *moi*? I have no money."

I've been meaning to look for a summer job, but Dad hasn't pushed the issue, so I really haven't looked that hard.

My brother picks up the nearest stuffed animal, the phallic-looking naked mole rat from *Kim Possible,* and starts tossing it up in the air, catching it like a football. "Do you know anything about the theater workshop they're doing this summer downtown?"

I try to grab Rufus away from him, but David keeps the naked mole rat out of my reach. "Um, I think they're doing *A Midsummer Night's Dream.*"

"I was thinking about trying out. Want to come with me?"

I stare at my brother, with his backward baseball cap. "Are you feeling okay?"

"I'm just looking for something to do this summer. I figured you knew all about that hippie drama stuff, so . . ." I think he is actually blushing.

Now I sit straight up as I continue to stare him down. "Since when are you into hippie drama stuff?" My brother is not really a hick. Far from it, actually. But he dresses like one and drives a monster truck that I tease him about mercilessly.

"All right," he says, setting the naked mole rat down. "You know Colton, who works at that coffee shop, the Pirate House?"

My jaw drops. "You've got to be kidding. You two are like night and day! He's like a goth queen!"

David has been trying to get me out of my room this summer, dragging me to his favorite coffeehouse in the city. I know I should be grateful to have a big brother who isn't afraid to let his little sister tag along with him, and I do like to sit and people-watch at the Pirate House. And it's next door to a wonderfully seedy looking comic book store. One day I'm going to get the nerve up to go in there.

"He sat in front of me in Composition last semester," David says. "He'd draw these funny little pictures on my notebooks."

"Is that why you failed that course? Are you saying it was the Queen of the Night's fault?" David just barely squeaked by his freshman year at the Savannah College of Art and Design, affectionately known as SCAD. My brother is majoring in architecture.

"No, but that's why I need your help. My English professor is directing the play. She'll kick me out of the theater for sure unless you come to tryouts with me."

"Me? Just because you got a bad grade in Comp One doesn't mean she won't let you work on the play. Besides, why would I want to go to play tryouts? I'm the antisocial one, remember?"

"Because you love your brother more than anyone else in the world." David sighs and fidgets with his cap. "I need you to come with me so I won't look like a theater dork. I'll just be there for my little hippie sister who can't drive yet."

He ducks as I throw Rufus at his head. "It's not like you have anything else to do this summer besides hide from the sun and sew weird clothes. Here's your chance to wear weird clothes on stage. If you don't want to try out for a part, maybe you could just work on costumes."

"Ooh, fairy dresses." I could have fun with this. Possibly. Except I really can't sew that well yet.

"And you don't want me to tell Dad about you climbing out your window and sneaking off to that bonfire with your weird friends."

I sit straight up in my bed. "How do you know about that? You weren't even in Athens at the time." If I hadn't snuck out that night with Caleb, I probably wouldn't have ended up in Winter Oaks.

David rolls his eyes. "I'm the big brother. I know more about sneaking out than you. So, are you coming?"

He does not know everything about my bonfire story. If he did, he'd know what Caleb did that night, and David wouldn't ask me to help set him up with anyone like Colton. Straight or otherwise, bad boys really can be bad for you.

Still, the theater workshop sounds interesting. And even though I've never been in a play before, I do love Shakespeare. Even madwomen have to leave their attics sometimes.

"When are tryouts?" I finally ask.

My brother grins. He knows he's got me. "Tomorrow at three."

"Tomorrow?" What am I going to wear? My stomach starts hurting already.

"You'll do great, I know it." David pats me on the knee, then jumps up before I can hit him with the naked mole rat again.

I flop back on my bed, listening to him stomp down the stairs and out the door, back to his dorm. I missed him so much when he left for college last year, and we still lived in

Athens. But Mom and Dad and I had to move to Savannah last month to be here with Grandma after Grandpa died. She refuses to take her psych meds anymore, and before Grandpa was even buried, the cops had already called Dad, when they found Grandma trying to set the house on fire.

She claims she was cold and thought she was lighting the fireplace. Why she thought she needed a fire in the middle of May, I can't understand. It's extra-hot up here in the attic, and even though Dad promises to get me a small window-unit air conditioner, it's not on the top of his list of priorities right now.

My parents are under way too much stress this summer. Dealing with Grandpa's death, and Grandma's craziness, and all of this happening right after my misadventure.

I pull my damp hair off the back of my neck and stare up at the ceiling. George Harrison is singing now. A slow, sad song about his weeping guitar. Grandma prefers the later Beatles albums to their earlier work. The long-haired, hippie years. Dad is constantly throwing away her incense so she won't set the house on fire again.

I know it's too hot up here to light any incense, but it would certainly help to disguise the cat litter smell that permeates the whole house.

No, I can't hide up here in this attic all summer long. I have to get out and do something. If I have to try out for a play in front of a bunch of strangers, that's okay. David will be there. And maybe I can help him win the love of his life.

CHAPTER 2

The old Savannah Theater is in one of the revitalized areas of downtown. Built back in the 1800s according to Mrs. Green, it was closed for almost fifty years, until a community arts group begged some money from local businesses and got some state grants last year. The dragon lady, as David calls her, introduces herself and welcomes us to the Savannah Theater Summer Workshop. She is a tiny woman, dressed in a dark purple sundress, with short spiky silvery hair. She gestures grandly with elegant long arms as she tells us about the historical theater.

Mrs. Green is particularly proud of the new lighting system they installed in March. What they need next, I think, as I look around the dingy theater, are some new stage curtains. The burgundy velvet drapes are looking pretty grim.

Still, I love the ornate molding that decorates the walls and frames the stage. I can imagine this was a beautiful place back in its day. I glance around at the various clusters of kids sitting in the rows of seats. A group of little girls sit in the very front, chatting and flipping their ponytails back and forth. Their leader blows bubbles with her gum and looks very bored.

Up on the stage, a group of silly boys are practicing stage falls. Not that anyone would need to be doing stage falls in *A Midsummer Night's Dream*. A pretty brunette is laughing at them and practicing her English accent. "I say! Thou art too funny, y'all!"

Over by the little girls, I notice a baseball cap. Someone is wearing a baseball cap INSIDE THE THEATER. And Mrs. Green is saying nothing about it. Even David has taken off his cap. The boy sits reading, oblivious to everything going on around him. And I realize I know Baseball Cap Boy. It's Lucas . . . Something. Crap, did I know he lived in Savannah? I can't remember.

Lucas was a patient at Winter Oaks while I was there. We had a few group circles together. He's quiet and, from what I remember, a preacher's son. Lucas Grant. He was battling depression. And . . . a suicide attempt, I think.

"Hippie," David says, pinching my arm. "Let's sit over there." He nods toward the middle of the auditorium, where Colton and two girls are sitting. One of them has long black hair streaked with deep blue. She is intimidatingly beautiful. She glances up at us when Colton waves, and looks right back down at her phone.

I wave to the other girl, recognizing her from the counter at the Pirate House. Her pale blond hair has purple streaks. Starla smiles and waves back at me. Good. I won't be too scared to sit with this group.

I miss my friends in Athens terribly. But I don't miss Caleb. And I don't think I could go back to high school there, where everyone knows what happened to me. So in a way, I'm kind of glad Grandma had her psychotic episode and we had to move to Savannah. Thank you, Grandma.

From the other side of the aisle, Lucas glances my way, frowns, and turns back to his book.

Fine. I can pretend I don't know you either, Asshat.

"David!" Colton squeals. "What's up, baby?" We drop into the seats right behind them.

To his credit, my brother doesn't bat an eyelash. "I had no idea you guys would be here. This is great."

To my credit, I don't snort at this blatant lie. At least, I try not to. Blue-hair Girl looks at me as I try to choke back a giggle. "Are you David's sister?" she asks. "Are you trying out for the play? I think you'd make a great fairy queen. Your hair is gorgeous."

I can't help but blush. I've always hated my red curls. They never behave like I want them to, no matter what beauty products I buy or which salon I go to. I have hopeless hair. Not gorgeous hair.

"Raine, this is Natalie," Starla says, introducing us. I give her a grateful smile. "She's right, Nat. You could be Titania!"

I think I blush again. "I don't know if I could handle a big part like that. I'm really more interested in working on the costumes."

Starla rolls her eyes. "You're too nice, honey. If you want to be an actress, you're going to have to be much more aggressive."

Do I want to be an actress? I haven't given it much thought beyond this summer play thing. Starla seems dead-serious in her ambition. She is looking up at the ceiling, inspecting the new lighting system. "My pale skin tends to look better under warm-colored gels. I hope they don't use the blue lights on me."

"You just need to get out into the sun more," Raine says. She is inspecting the ceiling, too. A plaster medallion decorated with frolicking cherubs floats precariously above our heads. "I heard this theater is haunted," she says. "I wonder if we'll see any ghosts."

Before I can ask what she means by this, Mrs. Green walks onto the stage with a clipboard and makes some announcements about the summer production. "Cell phones off, children. For the first group, let's get Colton Green, Starla Hayes, and Natalie Roman up here," Mrs. Green says. "Let's see what you've got, people. Start on page five. And remember to speak loudly and clearly!"

But wait, I didn't put my name down for the auditions. Did I? I open my mouth to protest, to say that's not why I'm here. But I'm paralyzed.

David pats me on the knee. "Just go ahead and try it. You'll do great."

Starla smiles at me as she stands up, but it's not a friendly smile. "We're up!"

I don't want to disappoint anyone. I don't smile back as I stand up. I'm too nervous.

I pray my stomach will unknot itself by the time I walk to the front of the auditorium. I pray that I won't do anything stupid like trip up the stairs.

I haven't been on a stage since kindergarten, when our class performed *The Food Pyramid*. (I was the celery.) The stage lights aren't on, so I can see everyone's faces in the audience. David sticks his tongue out at me.

I tell myself, this is Shakespeare. You love old poetry. You can do this. And if not, what's the worst that can happen? No one will die, right?

Of course not, Nat.

And I do okay. Not that I think it's an Academy Award–winning performance, but I make it through my lines without stumbling and without Mrs. Green having to yell, "Louder!" more than once. I even glance up from the script once or twice to look at Starla while I'm reading and gesture with my hand. I hope I get bonus points for the gesturing.

Starla gets points docked for not spitting her gum out.

Colton grins at me flirtatiously. He is a beautiful boy with short black hair and black as night eyes, rimmed with just a hint of eyeliner. He reads well, too, with a wicked English accent.

"Good job, people," Mrs. Green says. "Next up, let me see Ferris and Raine." Raine smiles nervously at me as I pass her in the aisle. "Y'all did great!" she whispers.

"Thanks, good luck!" I tell her as I sit back down next to my brother. I'm so glad it's over.

"You did great, Colton," he says, ignoring me.

David reads next, with a few of the little girls I saw hanging out near Lucas. The little divas can act rings around my brother, but he does okay. He sits down on the end of the row next to me, as Mrs. Green calls the next group up.

"Would someone be a dear and go get me a Coke?" Colton pulls a dollar out of his wallet and waves it in the air. "My throat is so dry now."

"Sure," my brother says, hopping up. "Put your money away. I got it."

"My throat's dry, too," I say.

David looks at me and rolls his eyes. "All right. Be right back."

Starla giggles at me when he leaves. "Your brother's cute."

Colton is watching David's . . . ass? Even though he doesn't say anything, I think that's a good sign.

I don't know if I should tell Starla that she's not David's type. "Yeah? I suppose." My brother would make a wonderful gypsy, with his long red curls that he usually keeps pulled back under a Braves cap. He has only the tiniest hint of a goatee. So not the image of your average truck-driving hick. He broke so many girls' hearts in high school.

A cold draft blows through the theater, as if the air-conditioning has just kicked on.

"Hey," David says, handing us our Cokes. I would have preferred a Dr Pepper, but I keep quiet.

"Thanks, sweetie," Colton says. I hope he really does like my brother. I would hate to think I was doing all of this for no reason.

David and Colton begin chatting like long-lost friends, and since Raine and Starla have their heads together, plotting to take over the world for all I know, I try to watch what's going on up on the stage. But my mind must be bored.

It starts working in overdrive.

Those kids up on stage are really good. I don't think my audition was that strong, after all. The girl with the black ponytail uses an English accent and seems to be perfectly comfortable with iambic pentameter. The guy reading for Bottom actually juggles.

I can't compete with a juggler.

And I'm nowhere near as cute as the little five-year-olds. Maybe I should have worn fairy wings today.

I let out a breath and see Raine and Starla glance back at me.

They're whispering about my sucktastic audition.

My heart starts getting wound up, and my hands begin to sweat. Oh no. I'm overcome with a sudden sense of impending doom and must escape. Somewhere in the back of my brain, I think I know I'm having a panic attack, but the rest of my brain is in FLEE FOR YOUR LIFE mode. I stand up, grabbing David by the shoulder.

"Be back in a minute," I mutter, before climbing out into the aisle.

"'Kay." He doesn't even look up at me. He doesn't care anymore. He probably wants me to leave him and Colton alone anyway.

I try not to stumble as I walk up the aisle toward the exit. Everyone is watching me. I can feel their stares on me. Ugh.

I open the doors as quietly as possible, but light from the foyer still floods the darkened auditorium. *Draw even more attention to yourself, Nat.*

The women's bathroom off the foyer has a sign on the

door: UNDER CONSTRUCTION, PARDON OUR MESS! I'm not about to use the men's room, so I head toward the backstage area, hunting for the dressing rooms.

It's quiet back here. All the lights are off, so I move slowly with my phone out for a little bit of light.

It's actually too quiet. My ears begin to buzz. I feel relief when I see the women's dressing room door and push it open, making a slight squeak.

There are several toilet stalls and even two shower stalls back here. Good to know, I guess. I'm not in any hurry to get back to that crowd, but I would hate for David to say something smart-ass about me falling in.

I head back through the dark backstage area and see the back row of curtains move. The area grows chilly around me, and in the dim light I think I see a person standing there looking at me.

I don't know if it's someone auditioning or someone working here at the theater. "Sorry!" I say. "Just had to use the bathroom!"

The person doesn't say anything and I hurry past, anxious now to be back in my seat next to my brother.

I turn around just as I open the door to the hallway, but the person in the shadows is gone.

At the end of tryouts, Mrs. Green announces that she'll be making final decisions within the next two days. Practice will be from five to eight, Monday through Friday, with set building on the weekends. The performance will be in four weeks.

I feel a nervous little jiggle in my stomach. What am I doing here? Performances? In front of people? I lean over and whisper to David, "Maybe this isn't such a hot idea." I could be spending my summer at the beach instead of stuck in this moldy old theater.

"Don't give up now, or I'll have to tell Mom and Dad about the bonfire with Caleb."

I hate my brother.

As we stand up to leave, I tug on David's arm. "Look up there on the stage. Do you see the curtains moving? There was someone back there when I went looking for the bathroom."

"Where?" David asks.

"The curtains in the back. See how they're swaying?"

David takes a look on stage and frowns. "What are you talking about?"

"You don't see the curtains moving up there?"

He stares at the stage again. Then looks back at me. "Oh Nat." My brother sighs heavily, and glances around to see if anyone else is nearby, listening. "Not again."

CHAPTER 3

I look at my brother and get a sick feeling in my stomach. My gaze swings from his sad face back up to the stage. To the movement in the curtains my brother can't see. Crap. Why did I say anything?

David has his hand on my shoulder. "It's okay, Nat. Did you—"

"Of course I took my meds!" I whisper. No one is paying attention to us, though. Starla is playing with Colton's phone, listening to his music with earbuds in. Raine is talking with Mrs. Green up on stage.

"All right. Maybe I just didn't look fast enough."

"Whatever. Can we go home?" I don't want to be here anymore. It must be the stress from auditioning. If I was hallucinating about the curtains, maybe the person backstage wasn't real, either.

"Colton asked if we wanted to stop at the sushi place down the street. I know you like their soup."

I sigh. I really don't feel like hanging out with strangers right now. Getting to know new people and trying to keep them from learning you're a freak is exhausting. "Why don't you go without me? You'd probably make a better impression solo."

David looks concerned. "No, if you want to go home, I'll take you home. We'll tell them you have a migraine or something."

And he lies so beautifully, I think he'll make a wonderful Shakespearean actor. I manage a feeble smile at Starla when she and Raine tell me they hope I feel better soon.

Colton pouts. "We'll miss you two." But he's looking at David when he says this.

"See, I'm helping you play hard-to-get," I tell my brother, when we are in the truck driving back to Grandma's.

He grins. "I already got his phone number."

"David!"

"But I want to hear more about you. Did you meet any hot boys in the psych unit last month?"

I roll my eyes. And the image of Lucas in the theater flashes before my eyes. He is so not my type.

"Who's not your type?"

Crap. Was I talking out loud? "Um, there was a boy at Winter Oaks that I saw at the theater today. But really, he's not my type."

David glances over at me, his pierced eyebrow cocked up. "Sis, the last boy you dated went to jail for dealing drugs. Before that, the other one slept with half of your class. While the two of you were going out. Maybe you need a new type."

I shake my head. "I don't think hooking up with a fellow psych patient is a smart idea."

"Probably not." He shrugs. "But tell me about this crazy but hot boy you met."

I love my brother to death. "I don't really know much about him. He was at Winter Oaks for a suicide attempt, I think, though he kept telling the counselors it was an accident. Obviously they didn't believe him, or he wouldn't have been there, right?"

"Hmm. Cute?"

"*You'd* think he was." Lucas has floppy blond hair that usually hangs over his face. When it's not hiding under a baseball cap. "Dresses like he belongs on the CW."

David's second "Hmmm" goes up an octave.

"Oh, but he definitely doesn't swing for your team. I just remembered the reason he tried to kill himself was because of his girlfriend dumping him. So he's not the boy for you, and definitely not for me. Don't need someone that hung up on an ex."

"But you just said he claimed he didn't try to kill himself."

"He overdosed on pills and alcohol."

"Did he leave a note?"

I shrug. I guess I shouldn't make any judgments when I've never held a conversation with Lucas before. But as I don't have any plans to have any deep conversations with him at the theater, it doesn't matter. And really, I don't think he's cute.

Much.

"Hmmm," David says again. And I realize I've just spoken my thoughts out loud. Again.

My brother pulls up in front of Grandma's house. That's one thing we miss about our house in Athens. The driveway and the garage. David has to parallel-park between Mom's Accord, Dad's F10, and Grandma's dead Jetta. She said I'm welcome to drive it if I can get it to run.

I'm thrilled at the idea, but Dad says it will probably take a lot of money. I should have gotten a job this summer instead of volunteering to hang out at the theater for free.

"I'm going back to the dorm, Hippie. Tell Mom I'll probably be back over with my laundry tonight or tomorrow, okay?"

"Sure. But you might want to know she was planning to make tuna casserole for supper tonight."

He makes a face. "Right, tomorrow it is. Thanks for the warning."

I roll my eyes as I hop down out of his truck. "Later, Hick."

I head straight to the kitchen and pull my pill organizer out of the cupboard. Did I take my meds today? The kitchen timer goes off and Mom comes in to check on something in the oven. "Hey, sweetie. How were tryouts?"

A warm, citrusy scent fills the kitchen as she opens the oven door. Heavenly.

"I auditioned for a part," I say. Today's square is empty. I must have taken my pill after all.

"I'm so proud of you! Want to try one of these as soon as they cool? It's a new recipe. Blackberry and lemon."

"They smell good," I say. "They're not for a customer?"

She shakes her head. It's been hard for Mom, leaving her catering business in Athens to move in here with Dad's mom. She's saving up money to open a shop downtown, but I know she worries about leaving Grandma here unattended while Dad is at work. In the fall I'll be going back to school and David is in college. We can't be home all the time to watch her.

And it's not like Grandma wanted us here. She's still suspicious of everyone. Mom and Dad are under too much stress. I'm trying my best not to add to it.

"I shouldn't have bothered placing that ad in the paper. I've only gotten one call from it and that lady wanted one cupcake for her boyfriend."

"Wow. Eventually the people of Savannah will realize how lucky they are that you moved here," I say. It burns my fingers, but I grab a cupcake anyway and break it apart. Blackberry-and-lemon-scented steam hits my face.

"It smells like crap in here," Grandma says, shuffling into the kitchen. "What are you burning?"

I turn the cupcake over. "It's not burnt. It's perfect. Want one?" But I see Mom's already moving toward the garbage with the rest of the cupcakes. "No! They're fine!"

I sigh as the rest of the cupcakes hit the garbage can. I want to yell at Grandma for hurting Mom's feelings. But we promised Dad we wouldn't agitate her. Nobody knows what will set her off, and we really don't want the cops to come back out again. I thought Dad would die of embarrassment. Even if he doesn't know our neighbors yet.

I look at Mom, but she won't look at me. She's ignoring both of us right now as she cleans up the kitchen.

"I need someone to go to the store for me," Grandma says. "I'm out of coffee."

"There are two different bags up here in the pantry," Mom says.

"Those are the wrong kind."

"What do you mean?" I ask.

"I can taste the arsenic in it. I know the doctors tampered with it."

Mom looks at me, and I swear I've never seen her so sad. So old. "Judith, this bag came from the grocery store," she says patiently. "I don't think they're allowed to sell arsenic-laced coffee. How about if I make each of us a cup?"

Grandma snorts. "I think I'll just do without." She turns and shuffles back to her bedroom.

Mom sighs, and I don't know if she's relieved or just exhausted. Every day it's another little battle. Grandma thinks we invaded her house because we are working for the government. And she says the government knows she's not taking her meds anymore. She stopped taking them when Grandpa died six months ago.

Dad hasn't had time to properly grieve for his father, since he's been too worried about Grandma. And then I had to go and have my episode after the night of the bonfire. I never meant to add to my parents' stress. I'm trying really hard to stay okay so no one has to worry about me.

Besides, watching how Grandma behaves off her meds makes me certain I never want to miss a pill again.

"The cupcake was great, Mom." I cross the kitchen to hug her.

"Thanks, Nat." She holds me half a second longer than I hold her. "How about if we skip the tuna casserole tonight and order pizza?"

I grin. We don't have to let David know he's missing pizza. "Sounds good."

She orders from her phone and starts to clean up the baking pans.

When the doorbell rings, Grandma grabs me. Her fingers clutch my arm painfully. "Don't open it! They'll go away if we're quiet!"

"Grandma, no. It's the pizza guy. He has our pizza."

Her eyes are wild as she stares at me. "You don't know that. It's not safe out there."

"It's okay."

"Little girl, you're working with them, aren't you?" She backs away from me.

"No, but if you go hide in the kitchen I'll get rid of him."

Grandma narrows her wild eyes at me. She barely knows me right now. And she has a hard time trusting me. "Why don't you come in the kitchen with me?"

"Because I have to get the pizza. I'll be careful."

"Judith, come in the kitchen with me," my mother says, standing in the doorway. "I want you to tell me if this coffee is okay."

"I already told you it was poisoned."

"I found another bag. In the back of the pantry. Come take a look."

Mom hands me her wallet as Grandma goes to the kitchen. "Tip him extra for waiting, okay?"

I nod. As soon as Grandma is safely distracted, I open the front door. The doorbell has rung three times now. A very pissed-off boy stands on the front porch step with our pizza.

Lucas.

"I'm so sorry. We were upstairs," I start to explain.

"Whatever. I could hear you guys. Twenty-four, eighty-two."

I hand him two twenty-dollar bills. "Mom said keep the change. And sorry again."

He's still doing a pretty good job of pretending he doesn't know who I am. Or that I know who he is.

But the hefty tip perks him up. "Thanks, Natalie. Enjoy your pizza."

I'm startled by the fact that he remembers my name. "You're welcome," I say. But he's already heading back to his car, an old silver Cherokee.

He gets in and drives off without another glance.

Lucas Grant, international man of mystery. Or maybe not so international. Local man of mystery?

I take the pizza inside and set it down on the kitchen counter. Grandma has decided that the coffee is safer to drink than the soda in the fridge, so she's sitting at the kitchen table with a mug. Mom is setting out plates and napkins for us. "I got half with mushrooms for Nat and me and the other half without, Judith," Mom tells her.

"Good. I hate mushrooms."

"I know," Mom says patiently.

"Your father used to hate them, too," Grandma tells me. "Used to think they looked like dead frogs on his pizza."

"Ew," I say, picking one off my side of the pizza and looking at it before popping it in my mouth. "Ouch, hot!"

"Frog burn your tongue?" Mom asks, grinning. She grabs a slice without mushrooms and hands the plate to Grandma.

Grandma pushes herself away from the table. "I think we have some Catalina dressing in the fridge."

I give Mom a worried look. She shrugs, just as Dad walks in the door.

"Hi, gang," he says, stopping to kiss first Grandma, then Mom. "Pizza night?"

"Let me fix you a plate," Mom says. "Frogs or no frogs?"

Dad groans as he sits down, still wearing his scrubs from work. Dad is an ER doctor, and seems to work all the time these days. "Oh Lord, Momma, why did you tell them about that?"

Grandma shrugs and offers him the bottle of dressing.

"I haven't put dressing on my pizza in years," Dad says. "But it's really good, Nat."

Convinced it was a crazy-person idea, I watch as Grandma drizzles Catalina across her slice.

Dad grabs the bottle and pours a small puddle on his plate. "Want to try?"

I shake my head. "My frogs are perfectly fine, thank you."

We all hear the front door bang open and someone stomping through the front hall. "Hey, guys," David says, dragging his laundry bag into the kitchen. "You got pizza? Cool!"

Grandma slides two more pieces from the box to her plate before David can even get close. She's learned quickly that you have to hide your food from my brother. Dad smiles at me as I shrug.

David doesn't even make it to the laundry room, just leaves his bag of dirty clothes by the door and sinks into the chair next to me. "Mmm, mushrooms."

I slap his hand, but he doesn't give up the slice he stole from my plate. "I thought you had plans tonight," I say.

"Don't they feed you at college?" Grandma asks.

"My roommates ate all the food in our apartment," David says with his mouth full. "And no, my only plan is to obtain fresh, clean laundry."

"I'll start your first load," Mom says, getting up from the table.

"You're the best," David says, already reaching for a second piece. "God, I love Giorgio's pizza."

I wonder how long Lucas has been working at Giorgio's.

Grandma takes one more slice of pizza and grabs the bottle of Catalina and takes her dinner to her room. When we hear her door shut, David nudges me. "How is she tonight?"

"The coffee is poisoned and the pizza guy works for the government."

He nods. "So, business as usual."

"Pretty much."

"How about you? Have you seen your curtain-wearing ghost again?" he whispers.

"Of course not." I glance up, but Mom is busy clearing the table and Dad is checking e-mails on his phone.

"Do you want to take the rest of the pizza back with you?" Mom asks David.

I start to protest, but David shakes his head. "My roomies don't deserve free food. Derek ate my hummus last week."

"The nerve of some people," I say, rolling my eyes.

"I know, right?"

"At least let me whip up a batch of muffins for you guys."

"Ah no, Mom. They definitely don't deserve muffins. You send some of your treats, they'll be trying to move in here."

"You're ridiculous," Mom says, but she smiles at him. I think she's just glad she's got one sane child. One perfectly normal child, as far as she and Dad know.

"Nat, where's my black shirt?" David asks, following me up the stairs to my room. "I know I saw you wearing it last week."

Colton. If it weren't for the pretty goth boy, David would still be wearing Polo shirts and baseball caps. I dig the shirt out from my dirty clothes hamper and toss it down the stairs to him.

"Ugh, it smells like oranges."

"Orange and ginger," I say, coming down the stairs. "It's supposed to give me energy." At least that's what the lotion bottle says.

"It will have to go in the next load. Any chance you can throw this stuff into the dryer when it's done? I have to get back to campus. I'll come back tomorrow and get this last load."

"No worries." I follow him as he carries a load of clean clothes out to his car. "Did you get enough pizza?"

He throws his clothes in his trunk, slams it shut, and turns around to tug my curls. "Of course, Mom."

I roll my eyes.

He lets go of my curls, and his grin fades. "You just figured they've got enough to worry about, so you'll pick up some of the slack? Do some of the worrying for them?"

"Ha. Maybe you should be a psych major instead of an architecture major."

He shrugs. "It would probably be more useful, huh?"

"Not at all," I say. "People need houses."

I'm sure Dad would be thrilled if one of us had shown any interest in following his footsteps and going into medicine. But he and Mom have both told us repeatedly to follow our bliss. I think my brother is on the right track. But I don't know what my bliss is yet.

CHAPTER 4

I'm silent in the car as we ride to the theater a few days later. There's a squirming feeling in my stomach. What if I don't get a part and David is embarrassed? What if I do get a part and there are too many lines to remember? Why did I agree to this again? Right, I was blackmailed. But so what if Dad finds out about Caleb? It's not like I ever want to see him again.

"I bet Colton got the part of Puck. Or maybe Oberon." David says. "He's got that Puckish vibe, you know?"

I'm the only one he ever talks to about his crushes, so I just nod my head. He came out to me his senior year of high school, but he still hasn't told our parents. I keep telling them they won't be upset, but he doesn't want to give them anything else to worry about.

At first it was because of Mom's new business. And then it was because of me. And then because of Grandma. I told David maybe Mom and Dad needed something new to take their minds off these worries.

He pulls into the theater parking lot and I see Starla and Raine getting out of a blue Fiat. They are laughing about something. A pang of jealousy twists in my chest as I miss my best friends—we used to go everywhere together, too. I text Andria all the time, and she came to see me once at Winter Oaks. She drove all the way from Atlanta, where she and her mom now live.

My other friend Trista sends me silly texts and e-mails all the time to make me smile.

But the therapist is right. I need to make friends here in Savannah. I get out of the car and wave back at the girls when Raine sees us and waves.

A blond little girl wearing fairy wings is dancing by Raine's car. She runs across the parking lot toward me.

"Be careful!" I warn as she tackles me with a hug. There aren't a whole lot of cars here, but she still should have looked both ways before she ran.

"I like your hair," she says, looking up at me.

David smirks at me. "You have a fan."

"Thank you. I like your wings," I say, grateful that I've made at least one friend here.

"Caitlyn, get back over here!" Raine shouts. "Sorry, she likes to attack people."

I take Caitlyn's hand and lead her back across the parking lot. "Are you going to be the fairy queen?" I ask her.

"Of course not!" she says, looking at me as if I were crazy. If she only knew. "The queen is a grown-up!"

"She's five," Raine says. "She thinks everyone over the age of twelve is an adult."

David scans the parking lot, and I know he's looking for Colton's car. "Nope, you have to be fifty before you're an adult," he tells her.

Caitlyn looks up at him, her eyes wide. "That's not true."

"Come on, squirt," Raine says. "Let's go inside. David is just teasing you."

David sticks his tongue out at Caitlyn when no one else is

watching. She sticks her tongue out right back at him. Good for her.

We go inside the cool, dark building and everyone shudders. Except Starla. "Oh, thank God, they turned the air on today. It was so hot during tryouts."

I frown, distinctly remembering how cold I had been, but say nothing.

Caitlyn follows Raine down toward the front, then turns around in her seat to look at me. "Are you a grown-up?"

"I don't think so," I say. "Can't I be a little girl like you?"

She nods her head solemnly, then points at David, who has plopped down in the seat next to Colton. "But they can't."

Someone sits down in the empty seat at the end of my row. Right next to me. Caitlyn's face lights up. "You made it! Come sit with me!"

"There's no room," Lucas Grant says, glancing over at me.

"I can trade seats with her," I say, starting to get up.

"No, he can sit with you, I guess. That's my brother."

Raine turns around when she hears this. "Hey, Lucas. She had a peanut butter and jelly sandwich right before we got here."

"Thanks for bringing her. I wasn't sure I was going to get off work in time."

"No problem. Do you have my money?"

He pulls a folded bill out of his wallet and hands it to her. Raine's face lights up. "Payday!"

I sit quietly, listening to a dozen conversations going on around me at the same time, and try to sort everyone out. Caitlyn is Lucas's little sister, but Raine babysits for her sometimes. Colton and David are discussing Mrs. Green, the theater director, who also happens to be Starla's and Colton's aunt. Starla and Colton are cousins, who both happen to work at the Pirate House. And Starla is trying to convince Raine to ask

Peter out. Not sure who Peter is, but by the way they are talking and glancing around, he must be here somewhere.

Mrs. Green steps out in front of the stage, decked out in another very dramatic purple tie-dyed dress with matching dramatically purple sandals, and all conversations die down. She beams at us, like a queen gazing upon her subjects. She begins with a long speech about the magic of Shakespeare and explains the play in a nutshell. Theseus, the duke of Athens, is marrying Hippolyta, the queen of the Amazons. Hermia is in love with Lysander, but her father wants her to marry Demetrius. Helena is in love with Demetrius, but he wants to marry Hermia. Does this sound like a soap opera yet? When all the young lovers end up in the forest, they are at the mercy of the fairy folk. The fairies give a love potion to Lysander, thinking he is Demetrius, and he falls in love with Helena. The fairy queen, Titania, is given a love potion by her husband and she falls in love with a witless actor, who winds up with a donkey's head. Various and assorted wackiness ensues.

There will be three nightly productions, each night performed by an entirely different cast. Anyone not performing is expected to help backstage with props, costume changes, and lighting. Mrs. Green tells us we'll be reading through the entire play today. Bethany passes out copies of the rehearsal schedules and the stage crew schedules, while another girl passes out copies of the play script.

"I am pleased that we had such a wonderful turnout for auditions this summer. Let's go over some rules and then we can get on with the cast assignments, starting with Cast One. Theseus and Hippolyta will be played by Michael Graves and Raine Holly."

"Oberon will be played by Colton Green, and Titania will be played by Natalie Roman."

Raine turns around to grin smugly at me. "We knew it!"

My stomach twists inside. I am half-thrilled, half-terrified. I try to imagine the gorgeous costume I will wear as the fairy queen.

Starla turns around and smiles at me, too, but her smile isn't quite as friendly. "Congratulations."

"Hermia will be played by Starla Hayes, and Lysander by Ferris Black," Mrs. Green continues.

Raine bumps shoulders with Starla and they both giggle.

"Puck will be played by David Roman." Colton and David bump shoulders and giggle just like the girls did.

I turn to the quiet boy sitting next to me. "Did you try out?" Mrs. Green is still reading out parts.

Lucas Grant shakes his head and smiles at me. It dazzles me for a moment. "Yes, but I'm more interested in working on the set. Caitlyn wanted to be in the play, but she's never done one before, so I'm mostly here to keep an eye on her."

"That's sweet of you to give up your summer for her. My brother kind of twisted my arm into trying out. I wish I'd thought about just signing up for set work."

"You don't like acting?"

I shrug. "I've never done it before, so I don't know if I can do a good job."

"No pressure there. Winning a lead role on your first audition."

I slump a little in my seat, aware of a squirmy feeling still bubbling in the pit of my stomach. "Nope. None at all."

Mrs. Green continues. "Lucas Grant, Demetrius. Bethany Peters, Helena. Jackson Spears, Egeus."

Lucas looks surprised. Starla and Raine turn around to congratulate him. Caitlyn dances in her seat.

I shiver as the ancient air-conditioning unit comes on and I feel a blast of cold air. I must be sitting directly under a vent.

"I guess we're both going to be actors, whether we like it or not," I say. "Congratulations?"

Lucas sighs heavily and frowns. "Lord, what fools these mortals be."

I grin at him. "I don't think that's Demetrius's line."

He shrugs, still frowning at his script. "I really didn't pay much attention when we read this play in school."

I don't want to sound like a nerd, so I don't tell him I've read every single Shakespeare play. And most of his sonnets, too, which I prefer. I really don't like his tragedies. *Romeo and Juliet* is just ridiculous.

"You have a cat."

"Excuse me?" I turn and look at Lucas. "How did you—"

"I'm allergic to cats." He sounds even more annoyed. His eyes do look a little watery. And red.

"Zora was sleeping in my laundry basket this morning," I say. "She probably got cat hair all over my shirt."

Lucas gets up abruptly and disappears out one of the side doors.

"Fine, you don't have to sit next to me, if it bothers you," I say to the empty seat. For a heartbeat, my feelings are hurt. Which is ridiculous. Lucas is really, really not my type. He knows I'm crazy. And he's not even a cat person.

After reading out the cast lists for the second and third nights, Mrs. Green is almost ready to start Cast One's first read-through. She dismisses the other two groups until later in the afternoon. I focus on my script. Four pages before I have any lines. I take a deep breath.

I can do this.

Lucas reappears with a heavy military-style jacket. "Here. It will cover up the cat hair."

I put the jacket on, only because I'm freezing. "It smells old. Where did you get it?"

"Backstage, prop closet."

"Thanks," I say, snuggling into it. It's navy with golden

braid trim and huge gold buttons. "Epaulettes!" I exclaim, touching the gold fringe on the shoulders.

Lucas looks mildly concerned at my excitement.

"I want to be a costume designer one day," I explain.

"Huh."

I hope Mrs. Green doesn't notice me wearing the jacket.

Caitlyn, bored since she has no real lines, turns around in her seat to wave to Lucas. He puts a finger over his lips to remind her to be quiet and she nods. She's really well behaved.

I wonder about Lucas's family. What made him think life was so unbearable that he had to end it? What does Caitlyn know about his suicide attempt and hospital stay? I wonder if he feels like Winter Oaks fixed him. He seems content right now, watching his sister. Maybe not happy, but not really depressed, either. Of course, the doctors at Winter Oaks probably gave him a magic pill to fix him just like they did with me.

I'm almost certain they fixed my head and figured out the right medications for me, but sometimes I worry that I'm still not quite right.

Starla is squealing quietly in her seat over the fact that she gets to kiss Ferris onstage. Now I'm worried. I start flipping through the script. Titania has to kiss someone, too, doesn't she? Bottom. Peter Gill. That's who I have to kiss onstage.

"Peter, the Paste Eater?" Starla asks, giggling.

"Oh gross," I say.

And she's not talking about innocent kindergarten experimentation, either. She says she saw him eat paste in art class last year. An eleventh grader. Yech. And for reasons no one can fathom, Raine is still crushing hard on him. Which makes me feel bad for her, because during the first rehearsal it becomes clear he has the hots for Starla. Poor Raine.

That night I spend all my time at home memorizing my lines. David comes by to help, but since he and I don't really have a lot of scenes together he leaves to practice with Colton. I don't think that breaks his heart at all. Still, I need all the help I can get.

I can't wait to see our costumes. Titania is the queen of the fairies, so I will get to wear something sparkly, probably with flowers braided into my hair. So will David as Puck. He's secretly thrilled.

The twins, Hailey and Bailey, are playing my fairy minions, Peaseblossom and Mustardseed, along with Caitlyn, who plays Cobweb. The two Lily Pulitzer–clad miniature bow heads sit in the front of the auditorium looking creepy, and when Caitlyn joins them, they look like a trio of creepiness.

The play is going to coincide with the Midsummer Night's Ball, an annual summer event Savannah's Civic Club is holding the night after the final performance. The ball is a fund-raiser to raise money to finish restoring the theater.

And the drafty old building definitely needs restoring. On the second night of practice, the lights start flickering and going crazy.

Lucas checks the light booth, but no one is in there. Mrs. Green shrugs it off, saying it's probably faulty wiring. "But I thought the lights were new," Colton says. Mrs. Green gives him a Look.

"Maybe they didn't replace the wiring when they replaced the lights," Lucas says.

When we hear a *pop* up above our heads, the little girls shriek. They think there are wild Pokémon in the rafters causing trouble.

Poor Mrs. Green. "What are they talking about?" she asks.

"Pokémon," Peter explains, adding much more detail than Mrs. Green could ever want or need, about video game critters with special powers.

"Some of them have magnetic powers," Hailey says.

"And electric powers, too," Caitlyn chimes in.

Lucas slinks further down in his seat, pretending to be invisible. He won't catch my eye, and I feel bad for him.

Starla leans over and tugs on his shirt. "Hey, Lucas! Go help the girls catch the Pokémons!"

"Actually, the plural of Pokémon is Pokémon," Peter says.

"Gotta catch them all," Colton murmurs.

"What if it's a ghost?" I ask, trying to distract everyone from the Pokémon theme. I think Lucas's sister is embarrassing him.

Starla and Raine turn around to stare at me. "Why? What have you seen?"

David glances over his shoulder at me, frowning. I know all about embarrassing older brothers. But I ignore him. "Well, I thought I saw someone standing behind the curtains the other day."

Raine's eyes grow big, and Starla looks up at the balcony and then back to me thoughtfully. All discussion of Pokémon ceases. But now I feel like the center of attention. And I don't like it. Why did I open my mouth?

"Male or female? Old or young?" Starla asks.

"I couldn't tell," I admit.

Colton leans over David. "I've heard my aunt say there are rumors about this place. We should hold a séance."

"Seriously?" David asks, his eyes growing huge.

Colton winks at him. "Don't be scared, I'll protect you."

The girls wait for the end of practice before pouncing on Mrs. Green. "Do you know any ghost stories about the theater?" Raine asks.

The dragon lady sighs. "Oh kids, we'd be here all night if I told you all the stories about this place. But theater people have always been superstitious. They say if a theater goes dark, ghosts will take up residence. So we always leave one light on in the building, called the ghost light."

"I'm sure this theater has gone dark several times over the past two hundred years," Starla says.

Mrs. Green shrugs as she shuts down all the lights save one. "All old buildings have their stories. And a theater is a building specifically created to tell stories and manufacture illusion. But you never know. This was once a beautiful theater, and if I were a ghost, I can't think of a prettier place to haunt."

Most of the cast and crew leave, including Lucas and his sister. We walk with Mrs. Green through the dark foyer and she lets us out before locking up. "We start costume fittings next week. Good practice, kids."

Raine and Starla drag behind the rest of us, whispering about something on Raine's phone.

David hovers between me and Colton, asks me if I want to grab some food before we go home. Loud enough so that Colton can hear, but it doesn't sound like he's asking him out in front of his aunt.

I know my role. "Sure. Colton? Care to join us?"

He throws one patchouli-scented arm around me and the other one around David. "*Chica,* I'd love to. What are we craving, my dears?"

I try to get a look at David, but it's hard with Colton between us. "I don't know . . ."

"Mexican!" Starla says, as she and Raine catch up with us. "Come on, let's go to the new place by the mall."

"Ooh, yes," Colton says. And suddenly we are all going out to eat together. I would give anything to be going home to a frozen pizza and a bubble bath right now. But David looks thrilled so I smile and nod.

"Everybody needs to ride with me," Colton says. "We can drop you guys back off here to get your truck afterward," he tells David.

And now I'm stuck in the backseat of his Corolla with

Starla and Raine. Who are asking me more questions about the ghost.

"Did you feel any weird sensations before you saw it?" Raine asks.

"What made you look behind the curtains?" Starla asks, before I can answer Raine.

I shrug. "I have no idea. I don't think I felt anything. Maybe I was cold?"

Starla leans over Raine to whisper to me. "We're going to investigate this, and it's going to be fun. Raine's great-grandmother was a voodoo priestess and Raine inherited her old witch board. Tomorrow night we're going to sneak back into the theater after practice and find your ghost."

I'm having trouble processing everything Starla just said. Voodoo? Witch boards? Why am I stuck in the backseat of a stranger's car with these crazy people?

Her whispers don't escape Colton in the front seat. "You're going to need me if you think you're getting into the theater after Aunt Carol has locked it up."

"I don't want to get Colton into trouble," I say, even though I know it's not going to change anything.

"Oh honey," he says from the front. "This isn't trouble. Think of it as our civic duty to seek out ghosts. To make the theater safe for all of the rug rats."

Raine nods. Seriously? A voodoo great-grandmother? Maybe Starla is lying, but I can't be sure.

Colton laughs. "It's probably just some guy in a sheet trying to scare everyone off so he can find the buried treasure."

"Okay, Shaggy," Starla says. "Just keep eating those Scooby snacks and believe that if it makes you feel better."

I glance over at David, in the front passenger seat. He's too busy flipping through Colton's iPod to join in the conversation. I get no help from him.

This just has HORROR MOVIE—BAD ENDING—

EVERYONE DIES written all over it. Teens sneaking into a falling-apart building late at night to converse with the dead? What could possibly go wrong?

But if there really is a ghost, there's a chance I'm not as crazy as I sometimes worry. Maybe it wasn't a hallucination. I might not end up like Grandma after all.

In the dark, no one can see my fingers crossing. I look at Starla and Raine and take a deep breath. It scares me, but I attempt to smile anyway. "Sounds like fun!"

CHAPTER 5

I'm recruited to spend the night at Starla's tonight with Raine, so we can eat ice cream and plot our after-hours séance at the theater tomorrow. When I ask Mom for permission, her face lights up. She is thrilled that her daughter is no longer an antisocial hermit. She sends me to Starla's with a plate of the dark chocolate cupcakes she made today. They have coconut frosting on them and they taste like Mounds candy bars.

My new friend lives in a cute blue house out by Bonaventure Cemetery. Starla's parents are divorced and she lives with her mom and eleven-year-old brother, Chance. He looks appropriately disgusted by the invasion of older girls in his home, especially when Raine arrives with her pet draped over her shoulders. Sunshine is a seven-and-a-half-foot albino Burmese python.

Chance shudders and locks himself in his room.

I wish I could hide in there with him, but I pretend the snake doesn't bother me. "How cute!" I say, hoping the snake isn't a prop in any voodoo ritual she's contemplating tonight.

Raine loves the cupcakes, but Starla moans that they have

way too many calories. "You're killing me, Nat. Trying to make me fat on purpose?"

I apologize, thinking what a bitch I am to be sabotaging her movie star diet. I push the sugar bomb of icing off my own cupcake with my finger, ashamed for being such a glutton. I should probably be more sensible in my diet, too.

Starla is a huge fan of horror movies, and while Raine drapes Sunshine around my arms, her best friend gleefully rummages through a row of DVD cases under the television.

"Here, you need to move your purse," Raine says, tossing it onto the chair across the room before I can object. "Otherwise she might try to crawl inside."

I can hear my pill bottle rattle inside the purse as it hits the cushions, and I feel a fleeting moment of panic. My secret is about to roll out onto Starla's living room floor. Zyprexa. Ten milligrams by mouth every night. For the treatment of hallucinations.

But the bottle stays in my purse and no one else seems to notice. I do not want to have to tell my new friends what a freak I am. Not yet.

Sunshine twists around my arm and I pet her head carefully. She's actually kind of pretty, in a reptilian way. I wonder if she can sense my faster heartbeat. If she thinks I'm prey.

Oh no, she's wrapping herself around my waist and my breathing gets faster, too. I'm scared and I know that she knows it. Will she keep squeezing harder and harder until I can't breathe at all?

"She likes to hug," Starla says over her shoulder. "How about *Jeepers Creepers*?"

I can see my headstone now. It's going to read: HUGGED TO DEATH BY A PYTHON.

Raine shakes her head. "I just saw that on cable last night."

"You guys pick, then." Starla plops down on the couch and pulls Sunshine off of me. "Come see Auntie Starla, baby. How is my precious Snookums?"

I want to eat some of the popcorn in the bowl on the coffee table, but I really need to wash my hands first. Can't you get salmonella from touching snakes? Maybe that's what my headstone will say.

"Sunshine looks hungry," Starla says.

"No. She's already eaten this week," Raine warns. "*Annabelle?*"

"I hate dolls," Starla says. "I'm in the mood for something classic. Let's look on Netflix."

I love old movies. "Like *Gone With the Wind*?"

Raine and Starla look at each other for half a second before they both burst out laughing. Raine holds her stomach she laughs so hard.

"Oh my God, I love her," Starla says to Raine. I feel like an idiot. "Nat, I was actually thinking more like classic *Nightmare on Elm Street.*"

Oh. I feel even more like an idiot now. What made me think I could make new friends here in Savannah?

Raine throws a sofa pillow at Starla's head. "No, really. We don't have to watch horror movies. We should watch *Gone With the Wind*. I love old-fashioned romances."

"No, that's fine," I say, curling my legs up underneath me. Drawing back into my Natalie Cave. "I like horror movies, too." Sometimes. Kind of.

Raine has the remote control now and she's scrolling through Netflix. "We don't need Freddy Kreuger. This . . ." she says, grinning triumphantly as she finds what she's looking for.

"This will be educational."

Starla squeals. "Perfect!" She does a little shimmy-dance on the sofa with Sunshine.

Ouija.

Of course. "Oooh, I've been wanting to see this," I say, weakly. Probably not very convincingly at all. Worst actress ever.

"Awesome!" Raine bounces down on the couch between me and Starla and settles the bowl of popcorn on her lap.

I know there's some hand sanitizer in my purse, but it would probably seem weird if I used it on my hands before eating. But I could get sick if I don't.

"Oh, there are drinks in the fridge, Nat. Feel free to help yourself."

The kitchen. I can wash my hands in there. "Okay. Do y'all want anything?"

"Beer," Raine says.

Starla hits Raine on the shoulder. "She's joking. Chance will tattle on us like last time. Just bring us each a Diet Coke please."

I take my time washing my hands and try to convince myself I'm having a good time. Horror flicks—yay! Giant snakes—yay! Why can't I be normal and laugh at creepy things like Raine and Starla? I feel like I'm five years old again, afraid of monsters under my bed.

I ignore the six-pack of beer and a pretty-looking wine bottle in the fridge and find the Diet Coke. Armed with drinks for everyone, I go back out into the living room.

The doorbell rings and Chance comes flying out of his bedroom.

Starla frowns at him. "Who is that?"

"No one," her brother says. "Mind your own business."

I can barely set the Diet Cokes down on the coffee table before Starla dumps Sunshine in my lap and tries to beat her brother to the front door. They shove each other, but Chance gets there first.

"You ordered pizza?" Starla shouts over her brother's shoulder. "Hey, Lucas!"

Raine comes to my rescue, picking up Sunshine. "Come to Mama, sweetheart. Hi, Lucas!"

"Come on in for a minute. Want to see the new Mario game I have?" Chance has the front door wide open now and I can see Lucas standing on the front porch with two boxes of pizza. He looks tired, I think.

"Hi, girls." He sounds tired, too. He gives a little wave, but frowns when he sees me.

"Chance, you know he's not supposed to go inside people's houses when he's on the clock."

How do Raine and Starla know so much about Lucas? And why do I even care? I glare back at him, but now he's doing his best to ignore me.

Lucas shakes his head, but remains out on the front porch. "It's fine. I'm done for the day. I brought him one of the pizzas I'd made for myself. One's pepperoni and the other one is Italian sausage."

"You shouldn't have done that, Luke," Starla says. "Now what is Caitlyn going to eat?"

"She likes the sausage better. Here, Chance, you take the pepperoni."

"Thanks!" Chance scurries back to his room with his treasure.

Starla rolls her eyes. "We were going to make sandwiches."

"How about some baked manicotti?" Lucas takes another bag that was hidden just out of view and holds it up for Starla.

She squeals. "Oh my God, Lucas! You are the best!"

Raine *hmphs* on the sofa next to me.

"What is the *hmph* for?" I ask. "Does she have a crush on him? Does he have a crush on her?"

Raine almost chokes on her Diet Coke. "No, he's just being nice. His family has lived next door to Starla's for years."

I stare at him as Starla attacks him with a hug. He smiles, but Raine is right. He doesn't look like a boy being embraced by someone he has feelings for. He glances up into the living room and sees me and Raine. His smile fades.

"Do you know each other?" Raine asks, staring at me curiously.

"Just from play tryouts," I say. I feel my cheeks flush and wonder if she noticed that he's frowning at me. That he probably hates me. Just because I know his secret.

Starla is dragging him inside. "We're about to watch a movie, Lucas. Why don't you join us?"

No matter what Raine says, Starla must have a crush on him.

"Sorry. I've got to get home. Caitlyn is waiting for me." He rolls his eyes. "And Dad."

I wasn't the most observant person during my stay at Winter Oaks, and I was definitely not interested in getting to know any of my fellow patients. I realize I really don't know anything about Lucas. Except that he has incredibly sad hazel eyes.

And he was a psych patient. And he really doesn't like me.

Fair enough. I probably scare him just as much as he scares me.

Raine sighs. "He's still getting over a bad breakup, but I think they're better off apart."

I want to ask her more, but Starla shuts the door and brings a steaming container of heavenly scented pasta into the living room. She sets it down on the coffee table. "Let me grab some plates and forks."

"This was really nice of him," I say.

"Told you," Raine says.

Starla comes back and dishes everything out. She hands each of us a plate of cheesy goodness. "Someday that boy is going to find a girl who deserves him."

"Not you?" I blurt out, before my brain-mouth filter can kick in.

Starla shakes her head. "Lucas is like a little brother to me." She and Raine share a look. Raine shrugs.

"Be right back with more drinks," Starla says.

I check my bottle of Diet Coke and I'm about to say I'm

fine, but Raine stops me. "Her brother won't come back out here again. You're going to like this." She's grinning.

I have a bad feeling about this, but I smile back and try the manicotti. It's delicious. I try my best not to embarrass myself by getting cheese all over the place, but Raine is making a mess, too.

She grabs one of the napkins Starla left on the coffee table. "So, are you seeing anyone?" She drags the "Soooooo" out longer than necessary.

"God, no. No more boys until I'm a grown-up. A real grown-up, not like Caitlyn thinks."

"Oh, sounds like there's a story behind that," Starla says, coming back out to the living room with three newly opened bottles of Diet Coke. She sets one in front of each of us. "Details, please."

Raine says nothing, but she's looking at me with one raised eyebrow, apparently waiting for me to spill.

I sigh. More dramatically than I should. Really, there's not much to my story. Not much that I want to share. "I haven't had much luck in dating." In other words, I make poor choices. "My last boyfriend went to jail for selling drugs." And I ended up in a psych ward after he gave me drugs. But they really don't need to know that.

"Oh wow. A drug lord princess!" Starla says. "Cool."

For some reason, the ridiculousness of Caleb being a drug lord strikes me as hilarious. I burst out laughing. "You make it sound romantic!" Almost.

Raine shakes her head. "Girl, okay, that's just one guy. There are plenty out there who aren't drug dealers."

"At least a few," Starla says. "Peter—" She fake-coughs—"Gill—" She coughs again.

Raine blushes and throws a pillow across the room at Starla. "How about—*cough*—Ferris—*cough cough*—Black?"

Starla dodges the pillow. "Ferris and I are just friends. You know he's dating Maizy." One of the girls from the play. I saw Maizy and one of the other girls, Bethany, scowling at Starla while she was up on stage earlier tonight. Starla smiles and holds up her bottle of Diet Coke. "To boys who aren't drug dealers!"

Raine and I both pick up our bottles, too. "Hear, hear," I say, and take a drink, forgetting all about Raine's suspicious warnings earlier.

It does not taste like Diet Coke. Rather, it tastes like half Diet Coke and half turpentine. It takes everything I have not to spit it back out. My eyes must be bugging out because they both laugh at me.

"What did you put in that?" I ask. I used to know my alcohol pretty well, but this is one I don't recognize. Not sweet like rum. Not smoky like bourbon.

"Just a little something special to get the pajama party started." Starla knocks back half of her drink.

I know I shouldn't mix alcohol with my meds, so maybe I should just skip my pill tonight? I take another sip. It's not so bad after all. Not really. "Crown?"

Starla grins. "Good job!"

Raine is smiling, too. I feel the warmth all the way down my throat and it makes me smile, as well. I know I'll be fine without my pill for one night. It's not like I really need them anyway.

Just for tonight, I'll skip. Just for tonight, I can pretend I'm a normal teenager and get drunk with my friends. I'll go back on my medicine tomorrow and no one will ever notice the difference.

CHAPTER 6

So quick bright things come to confusion.
—*A Midsummer Night's Dream*, act 1, scene 1

I have the feeling if I hang out with Raine and Starla all summer, I could get into lots of trouble. Or have lots of fun. Or maybe both.

In some ways, they remind me of my friends in Athens. But they've been best friends for a long time, and I'll probably never get to know them as well as I know Andria and Trista.

But all the people at Athens High know about my time at Winter Oaks, and I don't think I'd go back to school there now even if I could. I'd like to keep everyone here from knowing about my schizophrenia as long as possible.

Peter is hanging out with us while we wait behind stage for our next scene. Raine grabs my hand and squeezes it. She wants to go to the Midsummer Night's Ball with him so badly, and I'm worried she might be desperate enough to resort to some weird voodoo potion if he continues to ignore her.

"Hey, Starla." He doesn't even see Raine standing there. "Are you doing anything tonight? Me and some guys are going to play video games at my house. Want to come over?"

Ouch. Not only does he allegedly consume paste, he has atrocious grammar. What does Raine even see in him?

Starla looks Peter up and down, checking him out. I guess he is sort of cute, in a short, impish sort of way. "That sounds like fun, but I've already got plans for tonight." She sends a loaded, questioning glance at Raine. Oh Lord, is she going to invite everyone to their séance tonight?

Apparently Raine doesn't want her to, because she frowns and gives the slightest shake of her head.

"Just the girls," Starla says. "Sorry."

"Cool." He nods his head and takes a swig of his Gatorade as he shuffles off. Starla rolls her eyes. When he's gone, she shrugs at Raine.

Frowning, Raine stomps off to the girls' dressing room.

"He'll come around," Starla says, even though Raine is already gone. Mrs. Green calls her to the stage for her scene with Lysander. Great. Ferris gets his chance to fawn all over Starla onstage because this is the scene where Puck reverses his love spell on Lysander and makes him fall in love again with Hermia. Ferris's girlfriend, Maizy, is pouting in the front row.

My next scene isn't for several pages, so I head to the dressing room to see if Raine is okay.

But she seems perfectly fine, texting on her phone and eating a bag of M&M's. She smiles when she sees me. "We're going to have so much fun tonight!" she says. "Colton told his aunt that we're going to be working late on the set, painting flats. She's leaving him the keys!"

"How late do you think we're going to be?" I ask. I'm hoping if I say I'm with David, my parents won't mind me staying out late. I'm not crazy about the idea of the séance, but I'm happy to have any reason not to be stuck in the house with Mom and Grandma. I don't even think Dad likes being at home right now. And I think Mom resents him for that.

Raine shrugs. "It would be best if we don't start until midnight. We can send someone out for food and we can eat while we wait for the witching hour." Her eyes get big and she picks up her phone again. "And I know the perfect person."

"No, don't take advantage of Lucas that way," I say, peeking over her shoulder. She's already started a text to him. "Besides, don't y'all get tired of Italian?"

She puts her phone down. "You're right. And he probably has to take Caitlyn home. But we'll figure out something. Maybe David will go grab us something?"

"Probably."

She unzips her backpack so I can peek at the wooden Ouija board. It looks like a handmade piece. Not the Parker Brothers cardboard that I'm expecting. "Pretty," I say, shuddering when I think about the movie they made me watch last night. It took me forever to fall asleep at Starla's house, because I was certain there were demonic entities lurking in the shadowy corners of her bedroom.

I don't think I would have gotten any sleep at all if it hadn't been for the alcohol.

"Come on, we'd better head back out there before Dragon Lady comes looking for us," Raine says.

We go sit down out in the audience next to Lucas and Caitlyn, who's begging her brother to let her spend the night with the twins.

"Please? I'll clean my room and feed Rufus before I go."

Lucas looks harassed. "But Dad doesn't know Hailey and Bailey's parents."

"But you do. Remember when you talked to their mom in the parking lot after auditions? And we saw them with their dad in the grocery store last weekend."

Lucas rubs his forehead and Raine giggles. "You know it will be fine," she says. "She needs a girls' night."

"Who's Rufus?" I ask Caitlyn. I'm kinda hoping she actually has a naked mole rat for a pet.

"My guinea pig. You can come home and meet him if you want. But not tonight. I'm going to Hailey and Bailey's."

"I didn't agree to anything yet," Lucas says. But his sister is already giving him a hug that almost knocks him over.

"I'll tell them we're bringing pizza. We can, right?"

Lucas sighs as she skips off.

Raine crosses her arms. "Well, if you're getting pizza already . . ."

"No," I whisper, elbowing her in the ribs. And Lucas looks up at me. Really looks at me, for the first time since Winter Oaks. Or for the first time, actually. I don't think he ever paid any attention to me there.

It makes me uncomfortable.

"What?" he asks, his hazel eyes wary. "Sounds like you two are plotting something."

"Well, we are. Actually," Raine says. She ignores me as I elbow her again. "A few of us are staying here late tonight and were thinking about sending out for some dinner."

"We're, um, painting some of the scenery," I say, and ignore Raine as she elbows me back.

"Right. We're painting the scenery. Want to join us?" she asks. "Pizza optional, but always welcome."

"I already told Mrs. Green I'd be happy to help with the sets," Lucas says, stuffing his hands in his pockets. "So, pepperoni or supreme?"

Raine grins and twists one of her black curls around a finger. Is she flirting with him? "How about one of each?"

"I can chip in," I say.

"We all will," Raine says, even though I know it hadn't even occurred to her. "Let me go grab my purse."

I get left alone here in the dark hallway with Lucas. "I need to get my purse, too," I say and turn to leave.

"Natalie, wait." Lucas puts his hand on my arm. And just as quickly, he lets go of me. He looks flustered as he runs his hand through his hair. "Sorry, I just wanted to tell you not to worry about it. I've got the pizza covered."

I shake my head, trying to ignore the goose bumps his touch left on my bare arm. "You shouldn't have to. We should all help out."

He shrugs. "As long as you guys don't get tired of eating the same stuff day in and day out, I don't mind."

"I don't think I could ever get tired of pizza. Although the manicotti was divine, by the way."

"Glad to hear it." Lucas smiles and something warm and fluttery twitches inside my chest as I watch him leave. My chest shouldn't be doing that.

My brother, David, decides to stay with us for the séance. Mostly because Colton is staying, too.

Lucas has returned, too, after taking Caitlyn home to get an overnight bag and then taking her over to the twins' house. He's brought a bag of chocolate chip cookies along with two boxes of pizza. He is the hero of the hour.

He looks surprised to see no one painting, but when Starla pulls out the Ouija board, he doesn't look upset. He shakes his head and calls us all crazy. "Ghosts can't be real," he says.

"There are more things in heaven and earth, dear Lucas," Starla says, patting him on the cheek, "than are dreamt of in your philosophy."

Lucas looks from one person to the other, with an adorably confused look on his face.

"Hamlet," I say helpfully.

"Of course," he says, going back to his pizza.

When we're done eating, Starla makes us all gather around on the stage while Colton turns off all overhead lights except the one, the ghost light. The curtains are closed, so it's quiet on the stage. Except for Raine's hushed snickering and Starla's giggling.

Colton says all séances need liquor, so he pulls out a bottle of Bacardi for us to pour into our drinks. David frowns at me, so I sigh and reach for another cookie instead. Starla puts some rum in my cup when my brother isn't looking.

Raine lights a white candle and sets it on the floor. "Sandalwood, for protection," she says, and then proceeds to rub a smelly oil on everyone's forehead. I try not to sneeze.

"Was your great-grandmother really a voodoo priestess?" I ask.

Raine shrugs. "Maybe it was her sister. Or my great-great-grandmother. Just an old family tale about how we got the spirit board."

In the dim light, I can just see Colton cuddling up a little closer to David. My brother is finally making some progress.

Starla places the board on the floor in front of the candle.

The spirit board is hand-carved from yew wood, with runes carved along the edges. "Do you really think it will work with this many people?" Lucas asks.

"Shhh," Starla tells him.

Everyone places a hand on the heart-shaped planchette and Raine begins to chant. She sprinkles some water on each of us. At least, I hope it's just water. "Oh spirits, hear us tonight! We come to you in peace."

Oh dear Lord.

David giggles. Colton elbows him.

The tiny piece of wood begins to travel, first in random circles all over the board, then in square angles.

The hair on the back of my neck stands up. Of course it could be because my fingers are just touching Lucas's on the planchette.

"Whom are we speaking with?" Raine asks.

I hold my breath and my fingers grow bone-cold. The

planchette begins to stop at letters. An *L*, then an *I*, then back to *L*, then *Y*.

"Lily," Starla says, her voice a little wobbly. Is she scared out of her mind, too? "How old are you?"

The planchette jerks, then slides down to the number 5.

"Aw, come on," Lucas mutters.

"Hush!" Starla says. "Lily, are you one of the theater ghosts who live here? How did you die?"

D-O-N-O-T-A-S-K. Lucas and I look at each other. Lucas is not smiling. Neither am I.

"Let's ask her something easy," Starla said. "Lily, will Raine get a date for the Midsummer Night's Ball?"

Y-E-S.

"Oh, wicked! Who is it?"

P-E-T-E-R.

"Wicked!" Starla says, squealing. "See? I told you it would all work out! Lily, what about Natalie? Who is going to ask her to the ball?"

My cheeks burn and I can't look up at Lucas. Not because I'm thinking about the dance or anything. But because I'm staring at the words being spelled out.

D-O-N-O-T-A-S-K.

"Why not?" Raine asks, shocked.

D-O-N-O-T-A-S-K.

My stomach hurts. And I don't think it's because of the alcohol. This isn't real. It's all a game. Oh God. I'm starting to feel myself freaking out. What if it is real? I really think I saw a ghost in the curtains.

Starla sighs and leans back. "All right. What else should we ask her?"

I refuse to look up, even though I can feel everyone's eyes staring at me. What's so ominous about the dance that the ghost doesn't want to talk about it? Or maybe she just doesn't know. Lily is only five, after all.

"I think we should thank her and close the board," Raine says. She sounds like she's getting uncomfortable. Possibly a little tired. Everyone looks a little spooked now. Except Lucas.

I try to focus on his calm face. How the hell can he be so calm right now?

There's a loud crash behind us and we all jump back. One of the flats tips over, landing on top of the spirit board and the candle. Luckily the candle blows out and rolls away. I don't know what would have happened if the flat had caught on fire.

Colton is now sitting practically in David's lap, his eyes wide with fear. Raine and Starla look shaken. "Someone didn't want us to make contact tonight," Colton says.

I help Lucas put the flat back up as we hear the back door open. I hope he doesn't notice my fingers shaking.

"Kids? What's going on in here?"

Raine hides the candle in her purse before Mrs. Green can see. There's nowhere to hide the spirit board. "Um, hi, Mrs. Green," David says, shoving Colton off of him. "We were just trying to talk to the ghost we keep hearing about."

She frowns, sniffing the air. I know she can smell the burnt candle. "Oh, I could have told you about the ghosts. What do you want to know?"

"Jeez," Colton says. "How many are there supposed to be?"

"Let's see. I know of at least three of them. There's the Russian actress and her baby. And the little girl."

"What little girl?" I ask, terrified now that my hallucination from last week has a name.

"Back in the 1800s, there was a circus troupe that performed vaudeville acts in the theater. Il Diabolo Malevolo was a Romanian gypsy whose two daughters, Lily and Rose, performed the high wire act. Lily fell and broke her neck onstage one night. It's her laughter you hear up in the rafters sometimes."

Everyone looks up above the stage and shivers. Raine and

Starla couldn't have known about Lily, could they? Maybe they've already looked up the theater history and were just trying to scare me. I have a sickening, twisty feeling in my stomach.

"She plays her little tricks, and can be naughty at times," Mrs. Green says. "What else would you expect from a five-year-old?"

CHAPTER 7

"None of that was real," Lucas tells me, driving me home. I don't even know how I ended up alone with him in his car, with David and Colton and the girls going Lord knows where. But I have a midnight curfew. And Lucas said he needed to get home, too. "Ouija boards aren't real," he says.

I'm shivering, despite the fact that it's a steamy 90 degrees outside tonight. The air conditioner in Lucas's car isn't even on. The car smells nice. Like pizza and Lucas's cologne. "But what about what Mrs. Green said?"

"Natalie, how much did you drink tonight?"

Damn. "It's not the alcohol. I wasn't drinking when I saw the person behind the curtains a few days ago."

"What are you talking about?"

I sigh. Part of me feels like I can talk to Lucas. Because he was at Winter Oaks, too, and like it or not, there's got to be some sort of psych patient bond. But the other part of me says no, I'm not sick anymore. And I don't want Lucas to think of me that way. Don't mention the hospital, Nat. Don't mention the antipsychotics.

"On the day of the auditions, I saw something behind the stage. I thought it was a person, but it disappeared into thin air. Mrs. Green told Colton the place is haunted, so I thought I might have seen the ghost."

"Have you seen this ghost again?"

I shake my head. "But tonight I could feel something on that stage with us. Could you feel anything strange? Did the hair on the back of your neck stand up?"

"Not really. But then again, I'm not always an observant person." He's frowning again as he turns onto my street.

I can't believe he remembers my address from the pizza delivery last week. Maybe he's noticed me after all?

"Natalie, does your brother know you're seeing ghosts? Have you told your parents?"

Lucas thinks I'm hallucinating. The warm fluttery feeling in my chest suddenly turns cold and hard.

"No, because I know what they'll think. And I don't want them worrying. They'll pull me out of the play, and I can't stay cooped up in this house all summer." He's parked behind my dad's car on the side of the street. "Besides, David does know. And he believes me."

I don't mean for that to sound hurtful or accusing, but somehow it makes Lucas sigh. I wait for him to say something like, "I believe you, too, Natalie," or possibly, "I'm madly in love with you, Natalie," but of course he doesn't. Because that would be ridiculous. So I open the door and get out.

Out of the corner of my eye, I see him reach for me. But then he pulls his arm back and it's too late. "See you tomorrow," he says, putting both hands back on the steering wheel. "Take care."

"Thanks for the ride home," I whisper, wishing I hadn't been so quick to hop out. Wishing the ride had lasted a little bit longer. Even when he's accusing me of hallucinating and being a lunatic, Lucas is really a nice guy.

Who deserves a nice, sane girl. One without issues. I have to keep reminding myself of that. "See you," I say.

He waits until I unlock our front door before driving off. I walk inside to find I'm in the middle of an onslaught. Grandma has literally backed herself into a corner in the living room and is screaming at my mom for stealing her notebooks.

"What have you done with them?" she shrieks. Lord, the neighbors can probably hear her. "You think you're so smart, stealing all of my thoughts. You think if you turn them in to the police they'll put me in prison and you'll be rid of me."

"Judith," my mom begs, in a totally non-confrontational way, "I didn't take your notebooks. I'm not giving anything to the police."

"You want this house all to yourself, but that will never happen. I'm never going to die, sweetheart."

The way Grandma calls my mother "sweetheart" sounds malicious. Mom sees me in the foyer and tries to distract Grandma. But I'm drawn into the drama anyway.

"You're on her side, too," Grandma says accusingly when she sees me. "You think she'll take care of you when you lose your mind? Ha!"

Mom looks like she's about to cry. "Where is Dad?" I ask her.

"Tell me what you did with my notebooks, bitch!" I've never heard my grandmother cuss before.

My mother doesn't even bat an eyelash, but I can feel an icky, tense energy filling the house. "We can look for them in your bedroom, Judith," Mom says. "I haven't seen them down here."

I pull my phone out of my purse and call Dad. His phone goes straight to voice mail. Where the hell is he? I wonder if I should call David for backup. I don't know what he'd tell Colton and the others, though. Mom and I should be able to handle this.

"Grandma, would you like me to help instead?" Mom obviously needs to have a break. She deserves a week in the Bahamas, or at least a weekend at her favorite hotel in Hilton Head, but maybe I can at least give her a few minutes.

My grandmother glares at Mom and then at me. Her eyes shift back and forth rapidly. The crazy is right there, beneath the surface. She might explode at any moment. "Did she tell you where she hid them?"

"I'm sure they just got misplaced," I say, going up the stairs and hoping she'll follow me. "Maybe I accidentally put your laundry on top of the notebooks yesterday. Remember? I left out the fabric softener like you asked?"

She's following me. That's a good thing. "I hate the smell," she mutters. "Reminds me of Jim."

Ever since Grandpa died, I think Grandma's had a hard time. She's not taking her meds anymore, and I don't think she's grieving properly. She didn't go to the funeral. She wasn't released from the hospital until two days after Grandpa was buried. "Maybe we should find a different brand," I say, opening the door to her room.

It's a mess in here. The laundry basket I brought up last night is turned over on the bed and clothes are strewn everywhere. There's an empty coffee mug on her dresser and another one half-full of cold coffee on her nightstand. I'm still shaking from her and Mom's confrontation downstairs.

Grandma pushes past me and starts pacing. She's forgotten to bathe again and the smell makes me want to gag. It makes her small bedroom seem even smaller. I stay in the doorway, ready to escape at a moment's notice. I don't think she's ever become violent, but right now I really can't trust her.

That realization makes me tear up. I lean against the door frame. "Maybe they fell under your bed?" I suggest, hoping my voice sounds normal. "Or behind it?"

"Only the rats live below," she mutters.

"There aren't any rats here," I say. We've all been taught to counter her hallucinations with quiet truth. Reassure. Reaffirm. And for me, I pray I never see the same things she sees. To tell her there are no rats is also me reassuring myself. Otherwise I might end up unable to sleep tonight in the attic as I listen to every noise this old house makes. "Want me to look under the bed?"

"They'll bite you," she says, but she makes no move to stop me.

I wish David were here. Or Dad. But I can brave the rats and God knows what else is under her bed all by myself. "Let me grab a flashlight," I say.

"Here," she says, pulling a heavy one out of her nightstand. She hands it to me and puts her hands on her hips, waiting. The crazy is still there, right under the surface.

I click the flashlight on and get down on my hands and knees. I hold my breath, almost scared to see what's under there. Socks, a dirty bowl with a spoon, books. Maybe a notebook. The flashlight's beam hits two green eyes and I shriek.

Grandma jumps behind me and climbs up on a chair as her cat hisses and darts out from under the bed.

"Nat?" Mom comes rushing into the room. "What's wrong?"

"It was just Zora. I'm sorry." My heart is pounding.

"The notebooks are gone," Grandma says, climbing down off the chair. She sinks down on the bed and lets out a sob.

"They might still be there," I say. "I need something long to poke under the bed so I can push everything out."

Mom goes back downstairs and comes right back with a broom. I get back down on my hands and knees and sweep under the bed with the broom. A pile of junk is pushed out from the foot of the bed.

Grandma jumps up. "Get out!" she yells at Mom. She doesn't want her to see her precious stash. "You, too!" she says, getting in my face as I stand up. I try to take a peek at the stuff I've rescued from under the bed. There's a notebook in that junk after all. "Now, please," she says, but not politely.

I grip the broom tightly, not because I think I need to hit her with it, but because I worry she'll snatch it away from me. "Okay, I'm leaving."

I follow Mom into the hall and the door slams shut behind me. Neither of us speak as we escape downstairs to the kitchen.

Mom takes the broom from me and puts it away before giving me a hug. I'm shaking from the confrontation. We cling to each other in the kitchen, and I promise myself I will never, ever, ever forget to take my medicine. I can't do that to my family.

Except I don't think I took my pill tonight, but I did have alcohol and I can't mix them, can I? Also, I don't want Mom to see me and realize I forgot to take it earlier.

Dad comes in and when he sees us holding each other like war orphans, he stops. "Is it that bad today?" he asks, half-joking.

Mom glares at him, ready to take her frustrations out on him. I grab a banana and a Dr Pepper from the fridge and retreat to the stairs. I am tired of all the fighting today. I don't need to be here for this battle.

"Where the hell have you been?" she asks quietly, but with ice in her voice.

"Working late."

"She won't bathe and she's attacked both me and Natalie tonight because she thinks we took her damn notebooks."

Dad sighs and I hear him set his laptop down on the kitchen table. "I don't know what you think I can do."

"You can be here for dinner, for starters."

"I told you I was working late. There was a three-car wreck with multiple traumas. I couldn't just leave."

I reach the attic and blink back tears as I close my door. Tonight would be a good night for Grandma to blast Beatles' songs on her stereo. She's probably listening to my parents fight, though. Does it make her happy? Does she feel any guilt for the upheaval she causes in this house? I was mortified when I realized how much I had scared my parents.

I don't even want the banana or the drink anymore. I get ready for bed, sneak to the bathroom to brush my teeth. I stare at myself in the mirror.

I'm looking for my own crazy, hiding right beneath the surface of my skin. I see heavy shadows under my eyes, but everything else appears normal. With a tiny sense of relief, I sneak back to my room before anyone sees me.

I sink down onto my bed, suddenly overwhelmed and exhausted. It's past midnight, and the séance seems like it was days ago. I pray I'm too tired to have any nightmares tonight. I don't want to dream about ghosts in the theater. Or Grandma's angry face. But most of all, I don't want to dream about being locked up at Winter Oaks again.

Tomorrow, I'll be sure to take my medicine.

CHAPTER 8

I wake up to the sound of Grandma, singing in the shower about Maxwell's silver hammer having a close encounter with her head. Loudly.

At least it's not off-key. I shudder and throw a robe on before going downstairs to the kitchen. Mom is making cupcakes. Dad has already left for work.

I pour myself a glass of orange juice and open my pill case. "I thought you were taking the Zyprexa at night," Mom says. "Because it makes you sleepy."

Busted. "I forgot to take it last night," I say.

Mom sighs. "Do you want to go back and talk to the doctor about the shots?" They have a new injection they can give you once a month that works the same as a daily pill. But I hate needles.

I shake my head. "No shots. I'll do better, I promise."

"I read that they're doing studies to see if they can space the once-a-month shot out to once every three months," Mom says. "That wouldn't be so bad, would it?"

"Maybe," I say. But I really, really hate needles.

Grandma's voice booms from the bathroom again. That silver hammer sounds deadly.

Mom shudders with a glance up at the ceiling. "At least she'll smell better after her shower."

I want to laugh, but I'm embarrassed for Grandma. At least I didn't withdraw so much I stopped caring about personal hygiene.

"I hate that she takes so much of her anger out on you," I say. "What would Dad do if you just got a job and told him you didn't want to stay at the house with her anymore?"

"I can't just run away, Nat." She pulls a pan of cupcakes out of the oven. Mmm, red velvet. "As much as I'd love to."

"But that's what Dad did," I say. "He doesn't even stay home during the weekends."

"It's okay," Mom says. "We need the money right now. And the extra shifts he's pulling at the hospital really help."

My stomach twists with guilt. I have no idea how much a two-week stay at a psych hospital costs, but I heard Mom arguing with the insurance company on the phone. They didn't pay very much of the bill.

To make matters worse, our house in Athens still hasn't sold, so Dad's still paying the mortgage back there. I miss that house. I miss our swimming pool. And my old room.

I know Mom feels guilty, too, since she doesn't have the catering business she did back in Athens, but it's not her fault. We're all trapped here in this situation.

Movement catches my eye in the front window. The kid who lives across the street is dribbling a soccer ball back and forth across his yard.

Mom stands behind me. "Have you given any more thought to signing up in the fall?"

I used to love soccer. Our team in Athens racked up shelves full of trophies, as division champions for four years straight. I used to think of my teammates as sisters.

That was before our coach was arrested for sexual misconduct with one of those teammates. And then there was the Incident with Caleb.

I turn away from the window with a sigh. "I can't, Mom. It will never be the same."

"But it might still be fun."

I shake my head. "I don't think so. Maybe I'll join the drama club." If I don't freak out during this play.

Mom plays with my curls. It makes me feel like I'm five again, and all of a sudden I want to cry. "I always thought of you more as an artsy-type person than an athletic type," she says. "Do you remember the fairy-tale comics you drew when you were little? The characters had the most amazing outfits. I still have the drawings."

The Natalie who played soccer and used to draw pictures seems like a different person. Just like the grandmother I knew when I was little is not the same person I saw last night, screaming at us like a wild banshee. The grandma I once knew was smart and beautiful and always giving me books about princesses and dragons. She was never overly affectionate—I don't think I ever saw her hug anyone—but I still knew she loved me.

Grandma comes down the stairs and I see Mom tense up. She hurries to wash the bowls in the sink while I drink my orange juice, slowly. I have practice later tonight, but if the Zyprexa makes me sleepy, I think I have time to take a nap. I go ahead and take the pill.

Grandma sees me and frowns. "Glad to know the side effects don't bother you so much," she grumbles. She looks a lot more like the old grandma this morning, dressed in a colorful sundress and wearing makeup. She pulls a coffee mug from the cabinet. "Good morning, Elaine."

"Good morning, Judith," Mom says. She doesn't offer to

make any breakfast for Grandma. She knows a) Grandma doesn't trust Mom's cooking, and b) she has never been a breakfast person.

Grandma brews herself a cup of coffee and sits at the table across from me. She's alert and normal-looking today. She also looks embarrassed about last night's drama. She won't apologize, though. She did that once, after the fire, and it was so awkward for everyone that now we just pretend these episodes never happen. No matter how difficult that gets.

"How is the play coming along, Natalie?" she asks.

"Dress rehearsals are next week," I tell her, eager to get on with the pretending that everything is normal. "I can't wait to see my dress. All I know is that it's lavender and sparkles. And that I have wings."

"Goodness, already?" Mom asks. "Do you know all your lines yet?"

I nod. "Tickets go on sale next week, too."

Grandma looks down at her coffee. She really doesn't do well in crowds. And I feel like I've said the wrong thing.

"But you all know you don't have to come," I add. "David would probably be embarrassed for you to see him in glitter and horns."

Grandma looks up and grins. "Shirtless? I bet all of the fairy boys will be shirtless?"

Ew. "Um, possibly?" No, none of our family needs to come see the play, now that I think of it.

With a weirdly normal-sounding chuckle, Grandma gets up from the table and refills her coffee mug. "Elaine, if you go out today, would you mind picking up a few things for me?"

Mom's face is carefully blank. "I'd be happy to."

"Thank you, let me go write a list for you." She disappears back upstairs.

They'll never be best friends, and I'm pretty sure Mom

hasn't let her guard down, but at least the outright hostility is gone for the moment.

Maybe the old grandma is back. At least for a little while. Which means there's still hope for the old Natalie, too.

When she comes back downstairs, David is here, with a basket of dirty laundry. "Nat, if you could wash these this morning for me, I'll get them when I pick you up this afternoon for practice."

"No problem," I say.

"Well, hello, young man," Grandma says. "You are just the person I'm looking for."

David's eyes grow wary. "I'll do what I can, but I'm in a hurry."

"I need you to look at the battery in my car out there. Poor Natalie has no wheels and that Volkswagen is just sitting out there getting covered in dust and pollen."

Grandma follows David out onto the porch. Colton is leaning against David's truck, looking moody and glaring at Grandma. "Look, your friend can help you."

As much as I want a car of my own, I dread the idea of driving Grandma's Jetta. I know she'll be expecting me to take her to Lord knows where.

"Grandma," David whines. "I thought Dad was going to look at the battery."

"You know damn well he doesn't know his way around a car engine. And I know for a fact that you do. Who installed the stereo Grandad and I bought you for Christmas two years ago?"

That was David. He really does know what he's doing when it comes to cars.

Colton is frowning at his phone. "David, we're going to be late. My shift starts at eleven."

"I'm coming. Grandma, I'll see what I can do this weekend. Love you." He waves and gets into his truck. "Nat, I'll be back at six."

Grandma puts her hands on her hips, and we both watch him drive off. "I tried," she says. "Maybe by next week we'll have us a mode of transportation."

I have no idea what she's plotting, but I nod and follow her back into the house. I have laundry to do.

CHAPTER 9

David picks me up for rehearsal later, and as we pull away from the curb, I think about the conversation I had with Lucas last night.

"Did you feel anything spooky during the séance?" I ask my brother. "Do you think there's really a ghost?"

He stalls by searching for a good song on the stereo.

"Or do you think I was just hallucinating?"

David sighs. "Honestly, I don't know. Last night, when we were there, with the candles and the smelly oils, it was easy to believe that there was a ghost talking through the board. But now that I think back on it? Rationally? I think we saw what we wanted to see because we were all drinking. Which, by the way, was seriously bad for you."

"I know. I really didn't have that much. Just enough so the girls would think I was like them."

"What do you mean? Why would you want to be like them?"

"You know. Normal. Not on medication. You didn't say anything to Colton, did you?"

David shakes his head. "Why would I? Not that I'm embarrassed by you, Nat. You know that. But you know I wouldn't have any reason to bring it up." He's floundering. Badly. "Still, normal is overrated."

My smile is weak, but I feel obligated to make him feel better. "Just stop, please."

He glances over at me, and I can see the relief in his face when he realizes I'm not pissed at him. Am I that fragile? Does he worry about me like we worry about Grandma? I keep smiling, but I'm no longer happy with my brother.

"Anyway, I took my medication today, and I'm not going to drink anymore. So, stop worrying about me."

"Fine. But I'm still not sure about the ghost."

"I guess we'll just have to have another séance," I say.

"Great," David says, with only a hint of sarcasm.

I climb up to the balcony to watch Cast Three's rehearsals. Hermia and Demetrius are onstage right now, plotting to run away from Athens. The jealous Helena is about to thwart their plans.

The short nap I took didn't help, and I'm yawning up here in the shadows. I wish I had some coffee.

There's someone hiding up here already. Lucas. I start to leave, to give him some privacy, but something in his face makes me want to stay. To cheer him up. "Why are you up here lurking?" I drop down in the seat next to him. He doesn't make a move to get up or run away, so I think that's a good sign.

He looks up at me, with barely a raised eyebrow. I see hints of that eyebrow peeking through his floppy blond bangs. "*'Ill met by moonlight, proud Titania.'*"

"Ha. I see no moonlight." I put my feet up against the railing in front of me, sliding down in my seat. Now I can't see the stage. But it doesn't matter. They won't be ready for Cast One for a while. "Avoiding the fairies up here?" I ask. And ghosts, possibly?

Lucas shifts in his seat, restless. His eyes follow the line of my (just shaved, thank God) legs. Is he checking me out? I wiggle my toes. I just painted them a metallic lavender last night. I thought it looked like fairy dust.

"If only. Caitlyn has been wearing her wings twenty-four-seven, and insisting on fairy sprinkles on all of her food. Even her macaroni and cheese."

"What are fairy sprinkles in the Grant household? Colored sugar?"

"Cinnamon and sugar." He shudders.

"Oh dear," I say. "Tell her fairies don't eat macaroni and cheese. Tell her they prefer oatmeal. Or toast."

"If Caitlyn could eat breakfast food all the time, she'd be perfectly happy. French toast, oatmeal. She loves all of it. But Dad doesn't believe in breakfast for dinner. He says it's unnatural."

I can't tell whether Lucas is joking or not. I know nothing about his father, so I don't know if I'm supposed to laugh or offer sympathy. Lucas is paying so much attention to the cast down below us, his face gives me no clue how he feels about breakfast for dinner. I glance down to the stage. Helena has appeared and is trying to talk Hermia and Demetrius out of running away.

Does he really like Starla after all? I guess I should find out before I do something stupid, like decide that I like Lucas. Not that I don't already like him, just a little. He's funny in a weird, quiet way, and even when he scowls at me, I don't think he hates me.

But I'm not so stupid that I'd do anything crazy like fall in love with him. Still, it would be a good idea for me to know what his feelings are. If he is secretly pining for anyone. He looks like he might be pining.

We share an uncomfortably long silence as the scene plays out below us. "Did Winter Oaks fix you?" I ask suddenly, before I can change my mind. I feel like we need to acknowledge this huge secret we share. "Because I think they fixed me," I add, when he doesn't answer right away. "At least I hope they did." I just want Lucas to know that I'm okay. He doesn't have to be afraid that I'm going to freak out on him. "And, of course, I'm not going to tell anyone that you were there."

He laughs. "Most of the people around here know already. But don't worry. I'm not going to tell them that you were there. I guess your brother knows, of course."

I nod. Even David doesn't know everything leading up to why I ended up at Winter Oaks. He and the rest of my family just assume I inherited Grandma's crazy genes. The drug screen that they did on me in the ER didn't show any traces of ecstasy.

"Yeah, I guess they did fix me," Lucas says finally, staring at his hands. "I was having trouble handling stress. And now . . . now I can handle it better. I have to."

"I'm sorry about your mom," I say. I could say I just lost my grandfather, too, but I know it's not the same. I wouldn't be able to function if my mom died.

"Thanks. It gets a little better every day. And I try to stay busy. It helps when I don't have to stay at home and think so much, you know?" He stretches his legs so they are propped up against the balcony, just like mine. "Sorry, I try not to burden anyone with my crap."

I think about Dad and how he works such long shifts at the hospital. "It's not a burden. Thanks for trusting me."

I really want to ask him more about Winter Oaks. About how he ended up there. But I'm not ready to tell him the details about my "incident," so why should I expect him to share? I'm trying to think up a nice way to ask, *By the way, did you really try to kill yourself because your girlfriend dumped you?* But before I come up with the right words, he stands up. "Damn. I forgot I was supposed to get something for Caitlyn." He practically climbs over me to get out of the balcony. "See you later, okay?"

That warm, fluttery feeling in my chest is gone. "'Kay."

He escapes from the balcony, not looking back.

I sit there after he leaves and listen to the voices down below. The empty space around me closes in and I feel so lonely. I forget that I came up here originally to be all alone.

Now the solitude is frightening. I wonder if I make Lucas nervous after all. If he thought the crazy girl was going to start hallucinating in front of him, or have a psychotic episode. Or maybe he just didn't want to talk anymore.

Andria and Trista seemed nervous around me when they visited Winter Oaks. They brought me a mocha from my favorite coffee place, but they didn't know the staff would confiscate it. Neither one of them knew what to talk about. They tiptoed around everything, waiting for me to ask them about their lives. How was everyone at school? Oh, they're good. How was Alex? Oh, he's great. How was Hank? Oh, he's wonderful.

Nobody volunteered any news about Caleb. And I didn't ask.

Mrs. Green looks around, with her hands on her hips. Then she looks at me for an uncomfortably long minute. "All right, everyone back to their places. We'll take it from Puck's lines."

Everyone scrambles into place and I wait for my cue.

"Fear not my lord, your servant shall do so."

I enter the stage, joined by my fairy minions. After I argue with Oberon and conveniently fall asleep, he drops the love potion in my eye and I have to lie here pretending to sleep through the next few scenes. Mrs. Green promises I'll have something soft, like a giant bird's nest, to lie in during the performance. I hope I don't look like Big Bird.

I curl up uncomfortably on the wooden floor through Lysander and Helena's lines, through The Mechanicals' rehearsal of their play within the play. Puck casts his spell on Bottom and the donkey head goes on.

Bottom frightens off the other actors and it's my cue to wake up.

"*What angel wakes me from my flowery bed?*" I ask, rising with a dramatic, regal fairy yawn. "*Come, sit thee down upon this flowery bed, While I thy amiable cheeks do coy, And stick musk-roses in thy sleek smooth head, And kiss thy fair large ears, my gentle joy,*" I say to the donkey head. Mrs. Green has decided Peter has to practice with the head on even before dress rehearsals so he can get used to it. And I guess so I can get used to it, as well. It's really kind of creepy.

Colton and Starla are laughing out in the dark audience. I know Raine is watching, as well. If I get too friendly with Peter, I might get turned into a frog by a jealous voodoo priestess in training.

Not that I really believe that Raine is training to be a voodoo priestess. And not that Raine has anything to be jealous of. Peter the Paste Eater? Ugh.

"*Scratch my head, Peachblossom,*" he says to one of the little girls. The little fairies hasten to follow his commands.

"It's Peaseblossom!" Mrs. Green shouts from the darkness beyond the stage lights.

"*Scratch my head, Peaseblossom,*" he repeats. Caitlin giggles.

"Titania, you are supposed to be besotted with your Bottom," Mrs. Green's voice grows louder as she moves toward the stage. "Show me how besotted you are! Let me see the love!"

I want to roll my eyes, but I try my best to stay in character. I smooth Peter's furry head, but there is no way I am going to kiss his fair large ears.

"Sleep thou, and I will wind thee in my arms. Fairies, begone, and be all ways away."

And away with the rest of you imps and spirits in this building, as well, I think, glancing up toward the lighting as I cradle Bottom's donkey head in my lap. I have to slink down to the floor and pretend to fall asleep, as well, so Oberon and Puck can find us in the next scene.

"Okay, we'll stop right there for now," Mrs. Green shouts. "Cast Two, get in your places, please. Good job, fairies! Good job, Titania. I am starting to believe you really are in love with Bottom! And Bottom, I want you to work on your lines. You'd better have them all down by tomorrow. Got that?"

"Yes, ma'am," Peter says, pulling his mask off. He hands it to Cast Two's Bottom.

I go backstage to get my purse when I hear a little girl giggling. There's no one waiting on this side of the stage with me. I look up at the ropes above me, and search through the curtains. Nothing, except for clouds of dust.

The hair on the back of my neck stands up again. I try to focus on my script and read my lines over and over, but I can't concentrate now. Is it getting colder back here or am I imagining it?

Icy hands grab my ankles. I shriek, almost tripping over myself as I try to push the curtains back. There's no one behind there. I pull the curtains all the way back so I can see behind the stage.

There's no one here.

My heart is pounding so hard I can feel it in my throat. Is it the ghost?

"Natalie?" Bethany and Maizy come running up backstage to see what's wrong.

"What is the problem up there?" Mrs. Green shouts. I see that the scene has stopped, and everyone is looking at me.

I'm horrified. EVERYONE IS LOOKING AT ME. I can't talk. I would feel stupid saying someone just grabbed my ankles.

"Sorry," I whisper. "I thought I saw a rat back here."

The little girls squeal and even Bethany jumps back. Maizy rolls her eyes.

Mrs. Green is not amused. "Settle down! Colton, do you see anything back there?"

He and David pick up prop swords and investigate the area.

I'm going to die of embarrassment.

"It's clear," Colton says. "Might be some rat droppings back here, or it might just be Oreo crumbs."

"That was us," Hailey and Bailey say.

Raine and Colton are talking with Mrs. Green. Starla helps me put the rest of the props away. "Want to go get some dinner with us?" she asks.

"Where are you going?"

"Don't know yet. Colton says Mexican, Raine says sushi. I'm really not craving anything in particular. Got any suggestions?"

I glance up and see Lucas walking out with Caitlyn. "How about IHOP?"

Lucas stops and looks up at us. I think he heard me.

Caitlyn definitely heard me. "Pancakes? Lucas? Can we go?" She tugs on his shirt. I don't know why that makes me jealous, but it does.

David shrugs. "I could eat some pancakes."

"Breakfast for dinner is always awesome," Colton says, as Mrs. Green leaves us to go call an exterminator. "I'm on board."

Lucas shrugs and smiles at Caitlyn. He can't say no to her. "Sure, why not."

Raine puts her hand on my wrist and pulls me back away from the rest of the gang and pushes me toward Starla's car. "We need to talk."

CHAPTER 10

"Are you okay?" she asks, her eyes wide and serious. "It wasn't a rat that made you scream back there, was it?"

Starla unlocks her car and Raine hops in the backseat. I get in the front with Starla.

"Nat, you can talk to us," Starla says. "Was it the ghost?"

"I honestly don't know. It all happened so fast." I really can talk to them. Not like David. Or Lucas. I feel so grateful. "But something cold grabbed my legs. Like two tiny hands."

Raine's eyes are even wider. Starla's jaw drops open in surprise. "Are you serious?"

"Holy crap," Raine says. "We need to bring the board back and do another séance."

"Or an exorcism," Starla mutters. "Maybe we shouldn't be messing around with that thing after all."

Is Starla actually scared? I didn't believe that girl was afraid of anything.

Raine is plotting in the backseat. "Maybe if we called those friends of yours."

"I know someone who does the haunted ghosts tours downtown," Starla explains. "Maybe they'd let us borrow an EMF meter."

"No way," Raine says. "Seriously? Have you asked if he knows any stories about the theater?"

Starla shrugs. "Thomas used to date my cousin. It didn't end so amicably with him and Colton, so I thought it would be awkward."

"True," Raine says. "And besides, he'd have to get permission from the Arts Council and probably your aunt, too. But if we can borrow the equipment, we can say we're staying late to work on the set again."

"Let's think about this," Starla says, as she pulls into the parking lot. "If it's a little girl ghost, she can't harm us, right? And maybe we should talk to her again to find out what we can do to help her. You know, help her toward the light."

Raine rolls her eyes. "We need a cross and some holy water to help her. And someone needs to watch over Natalie." I turn around and she's looking at me curiously, her head tilted to the side. "It seems like the ghost has taken a special interest in you."

Now, that doesn't creep me out or anything. I try not to shudder. "I'm hungry. Are we going in?" I ask. Because bacon and pancakes will make it all better.

Raine sighs. "Fine. But we're not done talking about this. Don't worry, though. We'll make sure you're safe."

Something beeps on the floor beneath my seat. My phone must have fallen out of my purse. I reach my hand underneath the seat, but can't reach it. It's slid too far back.

"I've got it," Raine says. "Hey, your prescription is ready at the pharmacy."

"Oooh, is Natalie on birth control?" Starla says, pulling into the parking lot at IHOP.

"No!" I say, too fast. My cheeks feel warm.

Raine passes me the phone. "Don't tease her, ho. You know you've been on BC pills since you were twelve."

"Have not," Starla says, grinning. "And whatever, we're talking about Nat, here. Not me."

"We don't need to discuss me," I say.

"You know it's not birth control," Raine says. "That text is for her crazy pills."

"What?" I feel sick. What will they think of me? I didn't want them to know just yet.

They both giggle. "No, it's her STD cream," Starla says, and they are having way too much fun teasing me.

Right. They're just teasing me. Because we're friends. I take a deep breath. They can't possibly know about my prescription.

IHOP is packed. It's senior-citizen-appreciation night, and this IHOP is also close enough to the interstate that there are a lot of truckers eating here, too.

I spot Caitlyn and Lucas sitting at a booth, across the seat from David and Colton. Caitlyn looks up from her coloring sheet and waves at me.

Starla squeezes in next to Colton. Raine pushes me toward Lucas's side. "There's plenty of room for us over here," she says. "Caitlyn's a little squirt."

"Hey!" Caitlyn says, frowning.

Raine gives me a bump and suddenly I'm mashed up against Lucas. "Oof. Sorry."

"No problem," he says, turning away from me.

My phone beeps again and I look down. Oh my God.

Raine leans over to peek. "Who's Caleb?"

My stomach drops. He can't be back. Not now. I don't need him in my life. I look back down at the screen. *R U there?*

No, I'm not. "Evil ex," I whisper.

"Want me to answer for you?" Raine asks. "I can tell him

you found someone new and you never want to talk to him again."

"Tell him she's having so much fun with the new boyfriend she had to get her birth control prescription refilled," Starla says with a wicked glee.

"Please don't!" I say, covering my face in mortification. My stomach is twisting into knots. Why did I think I'd never hear from him again? Why now, in front of all these people? In front of Lucas?

Starla grabs the phone from me. "Here, let me take care of this." She types rapidly. *Who is this? Why are you texting me?*

Raine leans a little closer to me. "Is there a story there?" she asks, nodding toward the phone in Starla's hands.

I shrug. "Not suitable for children," I whisper back, even though everyone at the table can hear us.

Starla hands me back my phone. "I told him this number now belongs to a forty-seven-year-old gay Elvis impersonator and that he was welcome to meet me in my van at the river for a private performance. I don't think he'll answer. You're welcome."

"What's an impersonator?" Caitlyn asks.

Colton raises one pierced eyebrow at her. "You know what an Elvis is?"

"Duh, *Viva Las Vegas.*"

Lucas's little sister is weird in the most awesome kind of way.

I don't think Lucas approves of the table conversation. He hurries to change the subject. "Cait, what kind of pancakes do you want? Blueberry? Strawberry?"

"Chocolate!"

"I want chocolate, too," Colton says, as Lucas frowns at him.

"Can't you at least pick the kind with fruit on it?" he asks his little sister. "So we can pretend it's healthy?"

"Chocolate," Caitlyn says. I guess she's kind of stubborn.

Lucas sighs and lets it go. The waitress arrives to take our orders, and I excuse myself. In the bathroom, I check my phone. No more messages from Caleb. Maybe Starla's trick will work. I resist the urge to text him back myself. Why now? I want to ask him. Why me? I text Andria instead. *When did Caleb get out of jail?*

But at the last minute, I don't send it. I delete the question, worried that it sounds like I'm still interested in Caleb. Which I'm not.

When I get back to the table, everyone is still waiting for their food. But it's too quiet. Colton is checking his phone. Caitlyn is still coloring. Everyone else is staring off into space, lost in their own thoughts.

Are they all deliberately not looking at me?

They've been talking about me.

I can tell by the way Raine is playing with her fork.

Starla is watching the waitress clear the next table. And Lucas is watching the television up on the wall.

David is rearranging the syrup bottles.

They've been talking about my illness. David and Lucas both know, so either one of them could have said something. And now everyone at this table knows I'm crazy.

"Here we go!" The overly exuberant waitress brings out the food and everyone looks up. I see David glancing at me before concentrating on his plate. Is that guilt in his face? He had to be the one to talk. Or maybe it was Lucas.

Starla eats the whipped cream off her pancakes first. "Did y'all hear Maizy say a news crew is filming us during the dress rehearsal next week?"

"No way," Colton says. "I hope they get a good picture of my horns."

"Are you going to eat?" Lucas leans over and asks. I look down and realize I've just been pushing my food around on my plate.

"Sorry," I say. "Want my hash browns?"

He shakes his head. "Just checking to see if you were still with us."

I nod and finish my pancakes. I picked the chocolate ones, too, just like Caitlyn. I'm still here. Worrying about a million things, but I'm here.

I feel Lucas's hand squeeze my knee for the briefest moment. All thoughts of everything else fly out of my head as I realize how close we actually are. It's like a comforting touch, a squeeze from one friend to another. At least that's what I think it was. It didn't last long enough to be sleazy.

Am I supposed to squeeze him back? Caleb was never affectionate unless he was high or drunk. Usually I was drinking, too, so I didn't mind.

On the way home, Raine slides into the backseat again, so I get in the front with Starla. "Driver picks the music," Starla says, blasting the stereo as she pulls out of the parking lot.

Everyone in the car is silent for a long time, the space filled with loud music. I can't stop thinking about Lucas.

"Taxicab confessions!" Raine finally shouts.

Starla giggles. "You have to go first. You're in the back."

"Okay." She thinks for a minute. "When I was in kindergarten I French-kissed a girl."

"Who?" Starla demands.

"That's a different confession. It's your turn."

I'm scared to confess anything. I don't want to let the wrong secret out. And it would be too easy, in this space where we're all sharing deep dark secrets. It would be so easy to tell them I'm sick.

Starla glances over at me and her smile is friendly. "Your turn, Natalie. Driver gets to go last."

Here is my chance to tell them about my illness. I want to tell them. Before they find out some other way. If they haven't already.

"My grandmother has schizophrenia," I say, chickening out at the last minute. "That's why we moved here from Athens. She got worse after my grandfather died, and she needs someone watching her at all times."

I can't talk about me just yet. But this is a step.

"Wow," Starla says. "That sucks."

"I'm sorry, Natalie," Raine says. "It must be rough on your parents."

"Is that why you broke up with Caleb?" Starla asks as she pulls onto my street.

"Not really. He was just a bad influence on me."

"Cool house," Raine says as we pull in behind Dad's car. He's actually home for once.

"It's Grandma's," I say. "Thanks for the ride."

Raine moves to the front when I get out. "See you tomorrow!" she says.

Starla waves and drives off before I reach the front door.

The house is silent when I get inside. No psychotic grandmother singing Beatles songs, no fighting parents. No Beatles songs blaring from Grandma's bedroom. It's a good sign. She must be asleep.

The dishwasher kicks on in the kitchen and I follow its sound. Mom is cleaning up after another day's worth of baking. She's getting more orders now, so business is starting to pick up.

"How was practice?" she asks.

"Fine. I went to IHOP with David and his friends afterward. We had fun."

"Is he coming in?"

I shake my head. "He didn't bring me home. Starla did." I lean over the counter to sniff the cupcakes that are cooling. Coconut and chocolate.

"And who is Starla?"

"One of David's friends at the theater. Well, her cousin is

one of David's friends from SCAD. And they're both in the play with us."

I pour a glass of water to take my medicine. Mom smiles. She looks happier, more at peace than I've seen her in a long time. I'm making new friends and I'm completely stable. I have given her one less thing to worry about.

CHAPTER 11

I wake up to Mom bursting through the door to my room. "Nat! What do you know about David's friend Colton?" She doesn't even bother to knock.

Oh Lord. I know lots of things. "Why?"

She drops down to sit on my mattress, not bothering to wait for me to scoot over. I have to pull my feet out from under her.

"Oof, this is uncomfortable. Honey, is David gay?"

Why am I stuck in the middle of this? I sit up slowly, rubbing my eyes in an attempt to stall. "What are you talking about?"

Mom folds her hands in her lap. "Grandma says her friend Agnes's son Colton is David's boyfriend. I told her that couldn't be true. Because I would know, right? David would have told us. Or you would have told us. Right?"

As long as I've been begging him to tell them, an evil imp inside me wants to tell her it's none of her business. David has always been the perfect son. Straight As, soccer trophies, never a discipline problem, never any teen drama. I was the troublesome one. Sneaking out with boys. Coming home tipsy. Having a psychotic break at the spring break bonfire.

"I think Colton is gay," I say carefully. "He loves your cupcakes, by the way."

"Nat, you know we won't be upset if David's gay. Of course I'd still love him. I'd just be upset if he didn't think he could tell us."

I know it's not Mom; it's Dad that my brother is worried about. But I can't tell Mom that. It's not my place to tell her these things. Even if Grandma has already spilled the beans.

Hateful woman.

I sigh. "I really don't know anything," I say finally. "Can I have a cupcake for breakfast?"

Mom gives up. "Your father would still love him, too, you know." She goes back downstairs, without a yes or a no on the cupcakes.

Grandma is in the kitchen, drinking her coffee. I guess she hasn't spread enough malicious gossip for the day. And anyway, how does she know about Colton and David? She doesn't hang out with any of her friends anymore. She never goes anywhere.

"Are you sure you should be eating one of those for breakfast?" she asks, watching me take a cupcake and put it on a paper plate.

She has no right to tell me what to do, and I'm not feeling very polite this morning. "Mom didn't answer when I asked. That means, while she might not approve, she didn't say no, and she's not here to clarify."

Grandma rolls her eyes. "In that case, hand me one, too."

Back in Athens, one of Mom's best-selling flavors was a triple chocolate concoction called Prozac, because you couldn't help but feel happier after eating one.

I wish I could make everyone happy that easily.

"Grandma, how did you know about David?"

She finishes her cupcake and wipes her mouth with a napkin. "He told me when he was twelve. When he came to Savannah and stayed that summer with your grandfather and me."

A whole year before he came out to me.

I can hear my phone ringing upstairs, but it stops before I get back to my room. I missed a call from Raine. I call her back and she's frantic.

"Girl, I'm desperate and I think you can help me. I'm supposed to babysit Lucas's sister today, but I have to ride with my dad over to Tybee. If Lucas says it's okay, can you watch her? It's only from two to six, after her summer camp lets out, and then you can take her to play practice with you."

"But I don't have a car," I say. And I really don't think Lucas will agree to let a fellow psych patient babysit his little sister.

Raine sighs heavily. "Okay, you have a license, right? I can leave my car with you, since I'll be stuck in a truck all day with Dad. Please? Lucas only has one other backup babysitter and Mrs. Tully is in the hospital."

Grandma must have returned to her bedroom, because now I hear "And I Love Her" blasting from downstairs. She is in a mellow mood today.

"What about Starla?" I ask.

"She's working at the Pirate House today. It's only four hours and he'll pay you twenty dollars. I know that's not much, but he really can't afford much more."

"That's fine," I say. "I'll do it. If Lucas says it's okay."

"Why wouldn't he? He'll be ecstatic that I solved his problem for him."

"Shouldn't his dad be the one handling Caitlyn's babysitting?"

"Lucas's dad hasn't been right since his mom died. Honestly, I would have expected him to attempt suicide before I would have expected Lucas to do it. And after Lucas came back from Winter Oaks, I guess his dad felt guilty for failing Lucas, too, and he just gave up."

"Gave up on what?" I ask.

"He gave up on everything." She sighs again and I can hear her exasperation. "Can you watch Caitlyn or not?"

"I guess so. If Lucas says it's okay."

"Thank you. I'll text him right now."

"No problem." But that is a lie. What if he tells her no and tells her why he doesn't want me watching his sister? What if he tells Raine I'm too crazy to be responsible for little kids?

I jump in the shower, afraid that Raine and Starla are about to find out what a weirdo I am. Because I'm certain Raine will tell Starla the moment she finds out. And then I will lose two more friends.

I don't know why I'm even bothering. I shouldn't even try to have a social life here. It will only be a matter of time before I slip and do something that will land me back at Winter Oaks. Or possibly someplace worse.

When I get out of the shower, the Beatles are still blaring. I check my phone and there is a single text from Raine. *He says okay!*

I sink down on my bed, half-relieved and half-scared out of my mind. What am I going to do with a five-year-old for four hours?

I decide to wear one of my Disney shirts—it's a picture of the stained-glass window from *Beauty and the Beast*—and wait for Raine to bring me her car.

I tell Mom about my plans for the afternoon. She looks worried. "Are you going to bring the little girl back here?"

And suddenly I realize what she's thinking. Grandma. I

can't watch Caitlyn here after all. There goes my plan for having Mom around as a backup babysitter. "No, I guess I'll have to sit with her at the Grants' house."

Raine brings her car over before ten. "Sorry about dropping all of this in your lap. Here are the keys, Caitlyn is at the summer camp on Pine, she gets out at two, and she will have already had lunch. Don't let her talk you into taking her to McDonald's."

"Does she have a house key?" I ask.

Raine shakes her head. "Her father is home, but Lucas doesn't want her hanging out around the house when he's not there."

"Okay," I say, regretting that I called her back this morning.

Still, this is for Caitlyn, and I'm happy to help. Maybe I can take her to the playground or the mall or something. It's going to be okay. I try to smile as I take the car keys from Raine. "Have a good trip."

"Thanks, Nat. You're a lifesaver!"

Raine's Fiat is easy to drive, and I find the summer camp fifteen minutes early. I wait in line with a bunch of minivans and SUVs. I feel weird. When the kids are released, Caitlyn runs and jumps in the car. "You're not Raine! You're the fairy queen!" she says.

"You can call me Natalie," I say. "Raine had to do something with her dad today, so Lucas said it was okay for you to hang out with me for a few hours."

"Am I your minion?" she asks suspiciously. "Do I have to do everything you say?"

I'm pretty sure it's a trick question. "Do you have to be Raine's minion when she watches you? She's not even a fairy queen." I sigh when I realize she's still waiting for my answer.

"As long as you don't do anything dangerous like play in traffic or run with scissors, we'll be okay."

"Can we go to McDonald's? I'm starving."

I grin. "I know you're lying, little girl, but that's okay."

She shrugs.

The playground at McDonald's is fenced, and there aren't any crazy people here. Other than me, of course. "Do you like nuggets or cheeseburgers?" I ask.

She wrinkles her nose. "Neither. I like the fries."

We get French fries and chocolate shakes and sit at one of the plastic tables outside. Even in the shade, it's hot, and I wish I'd picked the McDonald's with the indoor playground. But last time I babysat a two-year-old, he climbed up into the play tunnel and I couldn't talk him into coming out.

"Do you like being in the play?" I ask.

"Mmm-hmm," Caitlyn says. "The donkey head guy is kinda weird, though. Do you like him?"

"My character, Titania, is supposed to like him. But only because Oberon and Puck put a magic spell on her."

"Lucas doesn't like him."

"Why not?" I can't remember ever seeing them have anything to do with each other.

"I don't know," she says, pushing her fries away. "And he doesn't like Maizy, either, because she was mean to me and Starla told him that she was a drug addict. Can I go on the slide now?"

"Maizy was mean to you?"

"She yelled at me when I was singing the *SpongeBob* song. I don't think she really does drugs, though. I heard Mrs. Green talking on the phone yesterday and she told someone that she was sorry for the misunderstanding and that Maizy was welcome to stay in the play." Caitlyn stands up. "I'm going to slide."

"Sure." I look at the time on my phone. 2:25. I have no

idea why Starla thinks Maizy is a drug addict. Or why a five-year-old would know these things. Only three and a half more hours to go.

Of course, I can't keep a five-year-old hostage at McDonald's for four hours. When she's finally played enough and finished her shake and fed the rest of her fries to the birds (ugh), I decide we'd better go on to the house. Maybe Grandma will stay in her room.

"Ooh, you have a tall house," Caitlyn says as we pull up behind Mom's car. "I wish we had an upstairs."

"My bedroom is up top in the attic," I say as we get out. "Want to see it?"

"Sure. Ooh, a kitty. Does she bite?"

Not as much as Grandma does. "She's mostly friendly. Her name is Zora."

The minute Caitlyn sits down on the front step, the cat rubs up against her legs and purrs. "She likes me!" Caitlyn is ecstatic. "I used to have a cat, but Lucas is allergic so we had to give it away."

This poor motherless, catless child. And it sounds like she doesn't have much of a father around, either. Lucas is all she's got. No wonder he feels the weight of the world on his shoulders.

He's too young to be raising a five-year-old, I think. "Caitlyn, how old is your brother?" I ask.

She shrugs. "I'm five. I'll be six in December."

And that tells me nothing. "Does he go to high school?" I press.

"I think he should have graduated last year, but he got sick and had to go in the hospital. Does Zora know any tricks?"

I shouldn't be grilling Lucas's little sister for information about him. When the cat meows and scratches on the door, I unlock it.

"Come on. Did you know my mom is the best cupcake baker in all of Georgia? Let's see if she has some for us to eat."

"Does she make chocolate cupcakes?" Caitlyn asks, following me inside.

The cat darts inside and disappears down the hall, tired of the five-year-old's attention.

"Come back, Zora," Caitlyn wails.

In the kitchen, I see a plate sitting out with chocolate frosted cupcakes waiting for us. Prozac to drown our sorrows.

CHAPTER 12

Caitlyn and I are watching the Disney Channel in the living room when Lucas arrives. We both have stomachaches. She ate two cupcakes, on top of the fries and milk shake from earlier.

Mom answers the door and shows Lucas into the living room. Caitlyn gives him a chocolatey smile.

"Let's get you washed up before you go home," I say. "Come into the kitchen with me."

Mom tries to give Lucas a box of cupcakes to take home, and he tries to politely refuse.

"Mrs. Roman says her cupcakes make people happy," Caitlyn tells him, while I scrub her face with a wet paper towel. "We need to take some home to Dad."

Lucas blushes. I want to give Lucas, his dad, his sister, everyone in the whole world Prozac cupcakes. I wish making people happy was my superpower. The power to banish sadness.

"Well, in that case," Lucas says, taking the box Mom is holding out, "thank you very much, Mrs. Roman." He turns to me, handing me an envelope. "And thank you, Natalie. I don't know what I would have done without you today."

"You don't have to pay me for today," I say, opening the front door. "Caitlyn and I just hung out for the afternoon. It's not like I'm a professional babysitter. I don't even know CPR."

"Lucas can teach you," his sister says. "He's a lifeguard and a pizza chef."

Lucas rubs his eyes. "Not a chef, Cait. Just a delivery boy."

At some point, Caitlyn has managed to wrench the box of cupcakes away from Lucas and Mom has disappeared back into the house. Caitlyn skips across the yard to his Cherokee, and gets in the backseat. "'Bye, Natalie! Thanks for the fries!"

Lucas raises his eyebrows, but doesn't ask. "Thanks again."

We're standing so close on the porch, I can smell coconuts. Suntan lotion. He must have been working as a lifeguard today. He's wearing khaki shorts and a navy T-shirt. I try to imagine him in swim trunks and blush. "Anytime," I say quickly. "She's awesome."

"See you at practice tonight?" he asks, his eyes lighting up. With hope, maybe?

I nod. "I'll be there."

"Good."

And we have nothing more to talk about, so he shuffles back to his car and takes his sister home.

Mom swoops down on me as soon as I come back inside. "So? Tell me about Lucas. He's cute, and his sister is adorable. That was really sweet of you to refuse money for watching her."

I sigh. It's not like I can talk about him with anyone else. Not Raine or Starla, and not David. "He was at Winter Oaks with me," I say. And I want to add, AND I THINK I LIKE HIM, but I see the hopeful expression in her face fall.

"Oh."

"So I don't think either one of us is dating material right now," I hurry to tell her. "But yes, he's cute. And smart." And even more adorable than his sister.

Mom squeezes my shoulder. "He probably needs a friend more than a girlfriend right now."

As much as it kills me to admit it, I know my mom is right.

"Do you know why he was hospitalized?" she asks.

"They said he was depressed," I say. "But he doesn't act like he's depressed." And he definitely doesn't seem suicidal. Is he on Prozac or some other potent antidepressant? Maybe he's too busy to be depressed. Or maybe he's so busy he doesn't have time to be a normal teenager anymore and that's why he was depressed. Maybe he resents his mom for dying and his dad for not being a parent. I kind of resent his dad for not being a parent and I've never even met the man.

Grandma comes out of her bedroom and sets her empty coffee mug in the sink. "Bad news to be messing around with a fellow psych patient," she says. "How do you know what feelings are real and what's just his pills?"

I don't even know what my feelings for Lucas are right now. The thought that those feelings might be caused by chemicals is just depressing. Or maybe he just seems so interesting to me because he's forbidden.

Mom rolls her eyes when Grandma turns her back. "You're just friends, right?"

"Just friends," I say. Trying to convince myself there could never be anything more.

"And please tell me you're on some sort of birth control," Grandma says, on her way back to her room. "The last thing you need to do is breed little crazy brats."

"Oh my God! Can we not discuss my sex life right now?" Even if her warning isn't necessary, she's right. It's probably safer if I don't ever have kids. The possibility of passing on Grandma's crazy genes is too great. And I wouldn't want to wish schizophrenia on any child.

Why does my grandmother have to ruin everything?

After practice, I ride up to the Pirate House with David. Colton is working the late shift, so he doesn't have time to chat with David. My brother is pouting into his mocha.

David glares at a customer that Colton is smiling at. A pretty girl. "Quit acting so jealous," I whisper.

David sighs. "He really can't turn his charm off."

"He's a barista," I say. "He's supposed to be charming. Surly baristas don't get tips."

My brother is still pouting.

"David, are you ever going to tell Mom and Dad? You know, Grandma said something this morning to Mom. I don't think Mom believes her, but now she is wondering."

David almost spits out his coffee.

"Grandma said you told her before you even told me."

He shrugs, playing with his cup holder. "I was stuck with her all that summer. I didn't have you to talk to."

"What's the worst that could happen if you tell our parents? You know they aren't going to disown you. Or stop loving you. You know that, right?"

"Of course I do. But they have a lot on their plate right now. With Grandma. With you."

"I'm fine," I say, hurt that he's still using my fragile sanity as an excuse. "You need to talk to them. Before Grandma does."

"So, where are your friends tonight?" David asks, glancing around.

He's not so subtle about changing the subject. "Fine. Raine is with her dad, but I don't know where Starla is." She never answered my text when I asked if she wanted to meet us here. "How long have you known the girls?" I ask.

"As long as I've known Colton, I guess. Since my first semester at SCAD last fall."

"And Lucas, too?"

"Yeah, I guess. He and Starla were dating when I first met Colton."

My heart stops beating. It takes an eternity for it to lurch forward again. "They what? Starla is the evil ex?" I ask. That makes no sense.

David looks at me funny. "Didn't you know? Oh. Oh no, Natalie. You and Lucas aren't . . ."

I shake my head. "No. Of course not. I just, I just didn't know."

"It wasn't a bad breakup. They're still friends, obviously."

"But she dumped him right after his mom died!" I say.

My brother stares at me again. "I thought you didn't know about it."

"I didn't know it was her." Starla and Lucas. Why didn't Raine ever say anything? None of this makes sense. Can I trust David and tell him about Lucas at Winter Oaks? I know there are laws that they drilled into our heads while I was there, to respect the privacy of other patients. There was a girl there whose dad was the sheriff of a neighboring county. Not that I would have recognized her or her dad, and not like I would have told the media she was there. But the staff made a big deal over patient confidentiality.

I can't tell David. "Nat, amicable split or not, I don't think he's ready for a new relationship. He had to go away for a while after his mom died to get his head on straight. I mean, he's a great guy. He's stars above your previous stunners, but I don't think he needs any more instability in his life, you know?" My brother looks down at his drink. "And I don't think you're ready for a new relationship, either."

"Relax. Grandma told me the same thing this morning."

As he looks up at me, I wave my hands. "I know—relationship advice from her, right? Not that there's any truth to it. Okay? Stop worrying."

He has the nerve to look relieved. And he's not telling me anything I haven't already heard, haven't already thought. But it still hurts to hear it from my brother.

And to discover Starla, in the starring role of THE EVIL EX. Does Lucas still have feelings for her? Does she regret breaking up with him?

My head is killing me. I rub my eyes.

"Are you getting tired?" David asks. "Want me to take you home?"

"Only if you come inside and talk to Mom and Dad."

He rolls his eyes. "Or you could just walk home."

"I'm scared of the homeless people," I say.

Colton comes over to our booth and bumps David with his hip. "Scoot over. What are you two plotting over here?"

"Shenanigans," I mutter.

Colton's kohl-lined eyes widen. "Sounds sexy. God, this night is dragging on forever. What are we doing after I close?"

"I've got to take her home," David says. "Then I can come back and help you clean up."

"About to turn into a pumpkin?" Colton asks me. "It's not even nine o'clock."

"David wants to get rid of me so you two can clean."

"She's funny," he tells David. "Are you going to come to SCAD when you graduate, Natalie?"

I shrug. I always thought I'd go to UGA when I graduated, with Andria and the rest of my friends in Athens. Caleb. He wanted to major in business.

"Are you sure you're okay?" David asks. "You're looking kinda pale."

"Just tired. I'll see you later, Colton." I get up and throw my cup away to give them a few seconds of privacy.

I'm glad I never got any closer to Lucas. I'm really glad we're just friends, and that all we'll ever be is friends. Because I'm friends with Starla, too, and friends' exes are always off-limits.

David refuses to come inside the house and talk. Both cars are in the drive, so Dad is actually home for once. "They're probably already asleep."

"It's only nine," I say. "But don't get mad when Grandma outs you."

"Ha-ha. Do you think they'll believe her? They'll probably think she's hallucinating."

"Whatever." The fact that he's joking about her illness makes me irritated. I slam the door shut when I get out.

He rolls the window down and shouts, "Don't forget practice tomorrow. We'll probably be going out to eat afterward."

"Fine." I don't bother to look back at him. Zora is waiting by the front door again. I unlock it and she darts inside.

Mom and Dad are arguing again, behind the closed door of their bedroom this time. I can't make out what they're saying, just the angry tones of their voices.

My phone beeps again as I'm climbing the stairs to the attic. I dig it out of my purse so I can silence it before it wakes up Grandma. I don't want her to hear Mom and Dad fighting.

Hey Crazy Girl. U miss me?

I want to throw up. I never truly believed Starla's trick would keep him from bothering me again, but still, I had hoped.

I don't want to answer, but I need to make him stop. He needs to know I'm not interested in talking to him ever again. *Leave me alone, Caleb. We are through*, I text back.

I'm so sorry, Nat. We need 2 talk.
There's nothing to talk about.
Can't I see U?
No.
Where did U go? Your house is empty.

Far away. Forget you ever knew me.
I can't forget you, Nat.
Oh my God. *Get over it.*
R U still mad about the X? I'm so sorry.

I put my phone down and walk to the window. I don't want to deal with him right now. I don't exactly blame him for my psychotic break, but I might have made it through high school without a possible early onset of schizophrenia if it hadn't been for him talking me into trying ecstasy. I know I shouldn't blame him. I made the decision to take the stupid drugs. I'd been an official member of the party circuit in Athens for years. I should have known the risks. Especially to someone with fragile sanity genes like mine. But I was a fool for Caleb. I thought he loved me. I wanted to make him happy.

I get ready for bed and go to the bathroom to brush my teeth. I try to ignore the constant beeping of my phone. Before I crawl into bed, I turn the phone over to place it on silent.

He's sent me several more texts.
Natalie I miss U.
Natalie I'm sorry.
Natalie where did U go

I turn my phone off completely, wishing I could turn my anger off just as easily.

CHAPTER 13

I'm sitting on a stool backstage, waiting for my next scene. I have a while to wait, and Caitlyn and the twins are running around back here trying out their new wings.

Raine and Starla are on the opposite side of the stage, talking with Lucas. He doesn't look at her like she broke his heart. She doesn't look at him like she broke his heart. She almost treats him like a little brother.

Colton pulls a stool over and sits down next to me. He has his horns on and looks a little demonic. "Should we wave to your boyfriend?" He wiggles his fingers. His nails are painted black.

"He's not my boyfriend."

"Maybe not yet. Don't worry. Starla won't mind."

I want to laugh.

Colton cocks his head to the side and his horns almost fall off. "Oh shit," he says, grabbing them. "Well, okay, she'll mind. But she'll get over it, because Lucas needs someone nice like you. Starla is not nice. And she wasn't the right girl for him."

"I think she's nice," I say.

Colton laughs. "She told the manager at the Pirate House that I had a communicable disease when she wanted me to take her to Atlanta for a concert and I had to work."

"She was trying to help you get out of work," I say.

"She told him I had Ebola and that I should have been quarantined. He almost fired me on the spot for contaminating his business."

"Wow. You think she did it out of pettiness or misguided altruism?"

Colton laughs so hard he has to hold his stomach. "Whatever. I've already forgiven her. You are a doll, Natalicious." He hops down from his stool to make his entrance onto the stage.

I wonder if he and David talked about Lucas and me last night. Surely they had other things to discuss. I try really hard not to think too much about that. I wonder how Colton came out to his family, how they took it. He seems pretty comfortable in his skin.

"Did he seriously just call you Natalicious?" David asks, taking Colton's stool.

"Do I even want to know what that means?"

David shakes his head. "No clue. But it's kinda cute."

I slide down off my stool, as Oberon makes his exit off to the other side of the stage. Caitlyn and the twins run to join me for the next scene. Time to be Titanialicious.

This afternoon, we're rehearsing the scene where Titania is sleeping in the woods and Oberon rubs her eyes with the juice of a flower to make her fall in love with the first creature she lays eyes on.

I'm lying in the giant bird nest pretending to sleep and Colton is leaning over me. I'm trying not to laugh.

Then I hear a creaky noise above us in the rafters. With a loud *bang,* one of the lighting trusses comes loose and swings down toward us. "Watch out!" I scream.

"Hey!" Colton grabs me and drags me offstage before the

light rigging crashes to the floor. Sparks pop as some of the bulbs blow. Someone in the audience shrieks.

"Calm down, calm down," Mrs. Green says. "Are you kids okay?"

My heart is pounding and my legs feel weak, but I nod. I look at Colton. "Thanks."

"You saw it coming before I did." He squeezes my hand and I squeeze back as my brother and Lucas leap up onto the stage.

"Natalie! Are you okay?" Lucas asks. He pushes my hair back and stares into my eyes. It would be romantic, but I think he's just checking my pupils. He holds up his hand.

"How many fingers do I have up?"

I push his hand away, frowning. "I didn't hit my head."

"David, will you go get the building manager?" Mrs. Green asks, her hands on her hips. "We need to find out what happened up there."

"Those lights were fine this morning when we were up there," Lucas says. "Michael and I both checked after we switched out the gels."

"I'm sure you two did everything right. But we need to get an electrician up there to check everything out. Natalie, Colton, how are you two doing?"

"I'm fine," Colton says. "Nat's shook up, I think."

"No, I'm fine." I shake my head, trying to ignore the quivering jelly in my legs. I try to stand up and decide I really, really need to sit back down.

"What is up with this theater?" Maizy asks. "You'd think it was cursed or something. It's not like we're doing *Macbeth*."

"Shhhhh!" Mrs. Green says. "You never mention that name in a theater!" Just then, the theater director and the building supervisor show up. She pulls them over to the mess onstage and tells them what has happened. Maizy huffs off to her drama geek friends.

"Why can't you mention that name in a theater?" I whisper to Lucas. I shouldn't be standing so close to him. This is making it so hard to remember that we're just supposed to be friends.

"Drama people are superstitious," he whispers back. His breath tickles the curve of my ear. "You're supposed to call it the Scottish play. If you say its name in a theater, it's bad luck."

"Like this theater needs any more bad luck," I say, looking up at the lights. A tiny, vicious thought pops up in my brain. What if it wasn't an accident?

I try to ignore that wicked little thought.

"Seriously, Natalie, maybe you should go sit down somewhere."

Raine and Starla have managed to sneak backstage where Lucas and I are standing. Starla attacks me with a hug. "Thank God you're all right!" she says. "Lucas, why don't you get her something to drink?"

"Are you okay?" Raine asks.

"Natalie, the theater director says you and Colton should be looked over by a doctor to make sure you're both okay."

"I'm fine, Mrs. Green," I say. "No gashes or concussions. No blood. No broken bones."

"Colton?" she asks, more worried for her nephew, I'm sure, than she's worried about me.

"I'm fine, too," he says.

I slip away from Mrs. Green while she checks Colton's head for concussions anyway.

Starla is staring at the broken rigging on the floor. "Maybe we should do an exorcism of the theater."

"An exorcism?" I sputter. "Are you two serious?"

Lucas returns with a Diet Dr Pepper. "Here." He smiles shyly when I take the bottle and stare at it. "I remembered."

"Thanks," I say, gripping the cold bottle tightly. The fact

that he remembered, even when my brother never does, makes my chest feel warm inside.

"We can't just sit back and watch the theater fall down around us," Raine says.

I take a step backward and my ankle decides to wobble at the wrong moment. Before I completely make an idiot of myself, Lucas rushes forward and catches me.

"Are you sure you're okay?"

"I'm fine. Just a klutz."

He pulls me over to one of the stools on the side of the stage. "Here. Sit. You've seemed kinda spooked all day."

"Just tired." Caleb's text messages kept me awake for hours last night. Now that seems like the least of my problems.

"If Starla and Raine are freaking you out with the ghost stuff, ignore them. You don't have to hang out here after practice if you don't want to."

"Oh no, that's all just fun and games," I say, wishing I could believe it. "Just silliness."

"You're saying now you don't think a ghost grabbed your ankles the other day?"

I shake my head. "Probably Hailey or Bailey playing a trick." I look up at him. "You don't think there's really a ghost, do you?"

"Definitely not."

I slump down a little. He thinks I'm hallucinating.

"Lucas! Is this the flat you've been working on?" Starla says, peeking at the giant flat on the floor behind us. "It's incredible."

"That's for The Mechanicals' play at the wedding."

"It's awesome. Are you going out to eat with us tonight? Nat, you're coming, too, right?"

I twist the cap on my drink.

Lucas covers the flat back up with a sheet. "I can't tonight. Cait's had enough junk food this week."

If that's a dig about me taking her to McDonald's, it hurts. I'll get David to take me home. I slide off my stool and go looking for him.

Caitlyn finds me first, attacking me with a hug. "Did your mom make any more cupcakes?"

"Not today," I say sadly. Today was a strawberry and rhubarb tartlet day. She had an order for a bridal shower.

"That's okay. Can I come over next time she makes the chocolate ones?" she asks, adding in a whisper, "My dad liked them. Lucas did, too."

My cheeks grow warm. He's disentangling himself from Starla as she talks to Raine. He glances over at me and for just a moment I see that sad look in his eyes. I wish I could wipe the sadness away for him.

"I'll be sure to hook you up," I tell Caitlyn. "I think your brother is looking for you."

"'Bye!" She skips over to him.

I need to run to the little girls' room before David takes me home. The stalls are all empty, but out of habit I go to the very last one.

When I come out to wash my hands, I scream. Two tiny handprints, in what looks like blood, are pressed against the mirror. Something dark flutters in the mirror behind me and I shriek. My heart is pounding. It looks as if someone just ran behind me, but there's no one in the bathroom with me.

I head for the door and run into Raine and Peter, who are trying to come in. "Was that you?" Raine asks. "What's wrong?"

I don't even care that Peter shouldn't be in here with us. "I came out of the bathroom stall and found that on the mirror."

"What?" Peter asks.

I walk back toward the mirror. There is nothing there. Nothing on the glass at all.

"What is it?" Raine asks. "You look like you've seen a . . . oh no." Her eyes grow huge.

"There were handprints," I whisper. "Two little-girl-shaped handprints. In blood." Where did they go? I could swear no one was in here with me. "Are you okay?" Raine asks. "You look like you should go home and lie down."

Peter stands in front of the mirror, poking the glass with one finger. "Cooooool," he says.

The hair on the back of my neck stands up. "What?" I ask.

"Check out my sideburns."

Raine rolls her eyes. I sigh. I could have imagined the handprints. Am I just hallucinating? Or are there ghosts here who just want to mess with my head? I don't know which frightens me more.

"Hey. Are you really okay?" Raine asks. "I think I just want to go home." Peter stares at both of us. "There's really a ghost here, right? Cool."

Raine frowns at him. "Did you think Mrs. Green was making shit up?"

"I guess the building is plenty old enough. And I did hear that some kid died here years ago."

Raine nods. "Her name was Lily. She was with a circus troupe."

I shiver, and I don't want to look in the mirror again, because now I'm afraid I'll see the shadow again. Either there really is a ghost in the theater or I'm really going crazy. I'm not sure which scares me more.

"Want me to find your brother?" Raine asks.

"No. I'm not staying in here. I can find him. I'll see you guys tomorrow."

"Okay, be safe." She grabs Peter by the arm and drags him out ahead of me. He's going to the Pirate House with them tonight.

I find David out in the parking lot with Starla and Colton. "Take me home, please?"

"You don't want to get food with us?"

"No. I'm not feeling good."

Both Starla and Colton take two steps back from me.

I shake my head. "Not sick. Just tired."

David frowns at me for a minute. "All right then. Come on. See you guys in a bit."

In the truck, he frowns at me again. "Need to talk?"

"What? No."

"And I think you do. Nat, even Colton was shook up by that light falling. I buckle my seat belt. Honestly, I've already forgotten about the light. "I thought I saw something in the bathroom mirror and it really freaked me out. But I think I'm just tired. Or maybe my contacts are dirty."

"Nat . . ." The serious frown is still on his face.

"Yes, I'm taking my pills! Do we have to go through this again?"

He starts the engine. "Have you talked to Mom about this stuff? Maybe you need the dose changed."

"Or maybe there really is a ghost in the theater," I mutter.

"One that only appears to you?"

"You saw the Ouija board that night," I say. I hate when my brother makes more sense than I do.

"That was probably five drunken teenagers guiding it."

"You don't believe me, do you?" I ask. "You really think I'm unstable again."

David sighs. "I think it's a good thing you're going home and getting some rest. That's all I know."

CHAPTER 14

Today, we are hanging out at the pool where Lucas is a lifeguard. There's no getting out of it. Starla and Raine made plans over a week ago for a pool day, but we got rained out. Today I have no such luck. There's not a cloud in the sky and the high is supposed to be 96 degrees.

My medicine has a photosensitivity warning on the bottle. I'm not sure what will happen. TEEN DIES AT LOCAL POOL BY SPONTANEOUS COMBUSTION. Or maybe I'll just break out into a weird rash. TEEN DIES FROM EXTREME MORTIFICATION.

I pull out my one-piece from last summer, a racing tank with purple and black stripes. I have an old gray, long-sleeved T-shirt of David's from the 40 Watt Club that I wear as a cover-up. And I borrow one of Grandma's huge sun hats. It looks like something Audrey Hepburn would wear.

Raine and Starla burst out laughing when they see me. They are both wearing bikini tops and cutoff shorts.

"Come on," Raine says. "We need to grab breakfast on the way."

I've already had a piece of toast, but get a large Dr Pepper at the drive-thru. Once Starla and Raine are properly caffeinated and their sugar levels are sufficiently high, we hit the YMCA pool.

"I wish we had a membership to the Aquatic Center," Starla says as we cart our towels inside. "Their pool is covered."

I have to pay the daily nonmember fee here. Maybe my parents would get us a membership at the indoor pool. Then I could bring the girls there and I'd be the hero of the day.

But of course, Lucas works here. Not at the Aquatic Center.

He's perched up in the lifeguard chair, sunglasses reflecting the sun off the water. Starla and Raine wave to him and he waves back.

He's wearing a white T-shirt and swim shorts. And he looks utterly delicious. Why isn't everyone in love with him? I just can't believe that Starla would let someone like Lucas get away. And just because they used to go out, now he's untouchable to all of Starla's friends.

It's not fair.

"Okay, ladies." Starla takes in the crowd surrounding the pool. The water aerobics class for the elderly is just finishing up and they are exiting the shallow end of the pool. A few young kids are running around the splash pad with their moms gossiping nearby.

There are no other teenagers here.

"That is where we are going to sit," Starla points to a space near the diving board, with several deck chairs. There's a shirtless, sweaty staff member trimming the hedges just outside the fence.

"Perfect," Raine says, staring at the shirtless person with approval.

"He looks a little old," I say. Not to mention smelly.

Starla shrugs. "Only twenty-two. Hunter is in some of Colton's classes. Come on."

I guess it's not such a terrible age difference if she's already out of high school. But I know my dad would have a cow if I brought home a boyfriend that age.

I follow her and Raine and we stake our claim on the deck chairs, draping them with our beach towels. I'm so glad I was able to find a plain blue towel in Grandma's closet. I didn't want to bring my *Little Mermaid* one. This one was just as big and smells like Downy. I dig out my sunscreen.

"Nat, you're never going to get a tan if you cover your skin with that," Starla says, snatching my bottle of sunscreen away. "It's like SPF one million."

"You're pale as a ghost," Raine says. "Just try some of Starla's stuff. By the end of the summer you'll look like you spend your summers on a yacht in the Mediterranean."

"Hello, skin cancer," I grumble.

They both strip out of their shorts and Starla makes sure Hunter watches as she gets Raine to slather suntan oil on her back. She smiles and then flops down to ignore him.

Maybe it's Hunter that Starla has dragged us here for and not Lucas. I don't know if that makes me feel better or not.

"Sunshine would love it out here," Raine sighs. "She likes to curl up on her hot rock in her tank and sunbathe." I shiver at the thought of a happy, sunbathing boa constrictor as Raine pulls out a paperback from her tote bag. "Want one?" she asks. "I have a couple of really good books in here."

"Sure."

"Here. Try this one."

I take the book she offers me and almost die from embarrassment. A naked man chest graces the cover. *Her Wickedest Desires*. Oh. My.

Raine grins at me before losing herself in her own book. I peek at her cover. *His Wickedest Dreams*. Oh. Dear.

I open the book she gave me and start reading, preparing myself to be bored. But the surly and studly hero has blond hair and sparkling green eyes. It makes me think of Lucas, even though Lucas's eyes are hazel. Sometimes they seem green and sometimes they look grayish-brown. I guess it depends on what color shirt he's wearing. I can't believe I'm thinking so much about Lucas's eyes. I try to focus on the pages in front of me.

I can't stop blushing as I read. And I can't put the book down.

I vaguely notice Starla getting up to walk over to the pool, where she dips her foot in the water. She comes back and sits back down, and before long I am lost in *Her Wickedest Desires* again.

But it's getting hot and I have to take my T-shirt off. Partly because of the sun, partly because of the steamy passages I'm reading. "Did you already read this one?" I ask Raine.

"Mmm-hmm," she says, never taking her eyes off her own book.

Starla squeals when Hunter jumps in the pool, his weed trimming finished for the day. His splash sprays all of us. I manage to save *Her Wickedest Desires* from drowning.

Raine's book is not so lucky. "You asshole!" she mutters, shaking her book out. The poor duke and his wicked dreams.

The water feels good, though. We couldn't bring our drinks out here, so I'm dying of thirst. "Is there a drink machine inside?" I ask.

"Right by the bathrooms," Starla says. And she jumps in the water with Hunter.

Raine sets her soggy book down to join them, but now I really must know what happens to the characters in the story I'm reading. The drink can wait.

I sit back down on my chair, even though my towel is damp now, and settle back in with the smutty book.

I tune out the splashing and the laughing in the water and get sucked back into the story.

I know it's silly, but I've already grown to care for the spunky heroine and I want her and the hero to find their happily-ever-after. The hero rescues the heroine from a house fire and she gives him a steamy kiss.

I need to fan myself with the book, it's so hot out here today. But I don't want to join the girls in the pool. I'm not the strongest swimmer and now they're playing Marco Polo. Hunter kind of reminds me of Caleb, so I have no desire to get in the pool near him.

I peek at the end of the book. I only have probably twenty or so pages left. I can read really fast if it's something I'm interested in. I go back to their steamy kiss.

I pull my hair back off my neck, and I wish for the millionth time today that I'd remembered to bring my sunglasses. The bright sun is burning my eyes.

Before long, there are spots dancing all over my line of vision. I keep blinking, but they won't go away. I feel a prickle of cold on the back of my neck, but the rest of me is still warm. Too warm. I don't think it's the book anymore.

I stand up, probably too fast, because I start to feel wobbly. I can hear the splashing and laughing in the water, but I really can't see them anymore. My hands tingle and my vision is closing in. I need to get out of the sun, but I'm afraid to move. I'm scared I might fall in the pool and drown.

"Natalie!" someone shouts.

The wobbliness takes over and the ground flies up to meet me. Ouch.

I hear more voices. And then shade looms over me. Lovely, cool shade. "Natalie," a voice asks. "Are you okay?"

I can't open my eyes. I think it's Lucas. My hero.

"Get her some water," Lucas shouts. Coconut-scented arms pick me up. "We need to get you out of the sun."

"I'm all right," I try to say.

"Your skin is on fire," he murmurs as he carries me inside to the air-conditioned exercise room.

I think that's the most romantic thing anyone has ever said to me. I think I might swoon.

Especially when he passes his fingertips across my forehead. "And it's dry," Lucas says. "Why aren't you sweating?"

"Here's some water," someone says. Raine, maybe?

Lucas props me up to a sitting position on the floor. "You need to drink this, but not too quickly. Go ahead and call nine-one-one," he adds to someone close by.

My eyes fly open, and I almost choke on the water he's trying to get me to take. "I'm fine. Please don't call anyone. Just let me sit here for a minute."

"Nat, are you crazy?" Raine asks, getting down in my face. "You just passed out. You need to be seen by a doctor."

Lucas is frowning. He asks Raine to get another bottle of water since I'm almost done with this one. Did I drink it too fast? As soon as she leaves, he stares at me. "Shit, Natalie. What kind of medication are you on? You're probably not supposed to be out in the sun, right?"

Of course he would know. I feel so stupid. He probably thinks I'm stupid, too. "Zyprexa," I whisper. And I shake my head, even though it makes my head swim. "But I was covered up."

"And you got overheated," he says, with a heavy sigh. "You have to be seen by a doctor, Nat. You know those meds increase your risk of getting heat stroke."

"Is she going to be okay?" Starla asks, coming up behind him.

I shouldn't have taken such a stupid risk coming out here today. My stomach clenches and I know I'm about to puke.

"I need to get up—" and that's all I can manage to say before all the water comes back up. At least I manage to turn to the side and not get Lucas.

Starla shrieks, jumping back before she is splashed. I'm so mortified, I want to die. "I'm so sorry," I say.

And suddenly the EMTs are here. I glare at Lucas. Even though I know I need to be seen.

They push everyone out of the way and start examining me, checking my temperature and hooking me up to a vital sign machine. The older guy asks me for a parent's name and phone number.

Oh God. "Please don't bother them," I say. "Dad's working and Mom has to stay at home and take care of my grandmother." Maybe they will just think it's just because I have a feeble, bedridden elderly grandmother. Not one who needs to be watched so she doesn't harm herself or others.

I feel a sharp sting in my arm and look down. The younger EMT is starting an IV. Maybe I am sicker than I thought.

"Sweetheart, you have a medical emergency," the older one says. "I'm sure one of your parents can spare the time to come down here and be with you."

I don't like the way he calls me "sweetheart," but I tell them Dad is a doctor in the ER at Savannah Memorial. I don't need to upset Mom right now. I don't want her to be disappointed in me again.

While the EMTs look me over and try to get in touch with Dad, I hear Lucas talking to Starla and Raine. Starla gasps. I think he's telling her about Winter Oaks. I see her glance at me and then quickly look away.

Raine comes back over to sit on the floor with me and grabs my hand. "Silly girl. Why did you have to go and scare us like that?" She looks worried.

The EMT is still talking to my dad. "Yes, sir. We're about to head out with her. Right." He hangs up and looks at me. "We need to get her on the stretcher."

"No, I can walk," I say, trying to get up without tangling the IV tubing. Raine stands up, too, and she and Lucas hold their hands out to help me.

But my legs wobble and darkness swallows me up again.

★ ★ ★

I wake up in a bed in the hospital. Dad is talking on the phone to someone. "I need to let you go. She just woke up. Natalie? Thank God."

I don't want to face him. I hate that I ended up here, through my own stupidity. Again.

"Nat, your mom is on her way."

"What? No! What about Grandma?"

"David is headed to the house. He said to tell you to hang in there. The doctor says you should be able to come home tonight. If your EKG is normal and your labs look better."

I look down and realize I've been poked again and now have electrode stickers all over my chest. The fact that I don't remember people doing any of this to me is frightening. "I'm so sorry," I whisper.

"Oh Nat," Dad says, sighing. "Do you know how dangerous this was? People die from heat stroke. Especially when they're on medication like you."

I can't stop the tears that well up in my eyes. Angry tears. And scared tears. "I'm going to be okay?"

My dad takes my hand. His fingers are cold, like he's been holding on to a soft drink bottle. "We don't think it actually was heat stroke. Just a severe case of heat exhaustion. So there shouldn't be any long-term damage to your organs." The pain in his eyes kills me.

"I promise it won't happen again," I sob. "I'll do better."

The curtain is torn back and suddenly Mom is here, pushing Dad to the side. "Natalie!" She pulls me into her arms, squeezing me tight. She is sobbing, too. I'm a terrible daughter for putting them through this.

A nurse comes in and hangs a new bag of IV fluids. Dad says they want to check my blood again after this bag is infused and then they will see whether or not I can go home.

Dad comes around to the other side of my bed, leaning down and kissing my forehead. "Okay, kiddo. I'm going back over to

Trauma now that your mom is here. I'll be back in a little bit, okay?"

"Okay."

Mom pulls the chair up closer to the bed and sits down. She sighs, and I know I'm going to get a lecture now.

"What happened?" she asks.

"I messed up. I'm sorry."

"Were you even trying to be careful?"

"I meant to. I was trying to. But I was trying to have fun, too, and I can't be thinking about my meds all the time."

"Oh Nat. Do you know how serious this is? You can't just hang out at the pool all day with your friends anymore. Not like before."

"I know. I'm sorry." I can't help but apologize. Over and over.

She stares at me, her lips pressed tight together.

"And I'm sorry you had to leave Grandma. Is she okay?"

"She's fine. Our neighbor Susan is sitting with her until David can get there. You know he'll probably tear you a new one when he sees you."

"Mom!" I glance at the curtain. Who knows who might be out there listening to us?

"Sorry. But he's pretty upset, too. Can't you see how worried we all are?"

Of course I can see that. And I hate that everyone feels like they have to worry about me.

I doze in and out, with Mom kissing me on the forehead at some point before leaving to get something to eat from the snack machines. Someone knocks on the door and I open my eyes, expecting to see the nurse again, but it's Lucas who enters.

"Hey."

"Hey." My lips and throat are parched, so it comes out

sounding more like a squeak. He looks so gorgeous, in his navy Polo that makes his eyes look so blue. I feel like a hag. My head hurts from crying earlier and I know my eyes are puffy. I want to hide my face under the covers.

"You really had us scared today, Nat." He's holding a bottle of soda, twisting the cap on and off.

"Sorry." My throat burns. I'm so sick of saying that word. "Sit down. Or do you have to go?"

He looks around, spots the chair, but then thinks better of it. "No. I didn't mean to disturb you. I just wanted to see how you were. And to let you know, I didn't tell the girls about your pills."

I close my eyes, relief sweeping over me. "Thank you."

"Well, it didn't seem to me like you wanted them to know. But keeping secrets like that could be dangerous. I mean, I understand why you'd want to. I wouldn't have told anyone about me and Winter Oaks if they hadn't been there when it happened. But they're my friends. And they're your friends now, too. Think about how they'll feel when they do find out. Don't you want to be the one to tell them?"

He's right, but I don't want to think about facing Starla and Raine right now. "But you were talking to them. And they were staring at me."

Lucas has the balls to smile. "I think they were impressed that your father is an ER doctor."

I close my eyes.

"You look tired," Lucas says. "I should let you get some rest."

My eyes fly open. For some reason I don't want him to leave just yet. "Thank you for coming to check on me. Thank you for everything. Especially when I did something so stupid I don't deserve to live."

His face blanches in pain, and I feel stupid all over again. I want to take my words back immediately. How could I have said something so idiotic? So cruel?

But instead of turning away, Lucas sighs and picks up my hand. "Natalie, you know that's not true."

And he's right. But I'm so tired of saying I'm sorry. So tired of apologizing. So I say the wrong thing. Again.

"Whatever. Maybe I do need to get more sleep." I turn my head toward the window, so I can't see his face. But he's not letting go of my hand. His thumb rubs against my wrist ever so gently. It makes my heart race and my chest tighten and my head woozy.

"Natalie." His shadow falls over me as he leans closer. "I wanted to ask you—"

The door swings open and Lucas drops my hand as my brother enters the room. "Hey, Hippie. I brought you some ice cream from Leopold's. Something to freeze your brain." He's holding a pint of my favorite ice cream. Mmm, pistachio.

David stops when he sees Lucas. "Hey, I heard you were the one that took care of her until the paramedics could arrive. You should go to med school or something."

"Gimme," I say, holding my hands out toward the ice cream.

Lucas shoves his hand back in his pocket. "Yeah, I don't know about that," he tells David. He looks back at me, his eyes somber. "Take care, Nat. I'd better go."

"See you," my brother says. He waits until Lucas leaves, then turns to me with a frown.

"Don't even start until I get that ice cream," I tell him. Pistachio ice cream will make any ass-chewing he plans to give me a little more tolerable.

He hands it over, along with a spoon he snagged from the nurses' station. "I'm not going to yell. I figure Mom probably did enough of that, huh?"

I look up at my brother in surprise, and the lump in my throat isn't from the cold ice cream. "Thank you," I whisper, afraid I'm going to cry in front of him.

He sighs and pulls the chair over to the bed, sitting down beside me. "It was incredibly stupid, but I think you know that. I'm just glad you're all right."

I nod, because I know that's what he wants. To think that I'm all right. But I'm so scared that I'm not all right. That I'll never be all right again.

CHAPTER 15

Two days before the dress rehearsal, Mrs. Green meets the cast and crew with a disgusted look on her face. Those baroque, golden cherubs decorating the proscenium above the stage do not look like they're smiling, either. They look downright malicious.

"Before we get started, I have a few short announcements to make. The Civic Arts Council has expressed concern about the safety of this building. I wanted to let everyone know . . . well, they are having a meeting tonight to decide whether or not to cancel the play."

There's a ripple of noise in the audience. "Oh, that bites," Starla says, kicking the seat in front of her with her boot. Maizy turns around and glares at her.

"Mrs. Green, what about the fund-raising planned?" Raine asks. "Don't they need this performance in order to receive the state grants?"

Mrs. Green sighs and shrugs helplessly. "The council is well aware of that. But I guess they're more worried about lawsuits from parents."

I look around the dim theater. Is this what the ghosts want? Are they trying to get rid of everyone?

"Now, I know a lot of parents have called me in the past week after the lighting accident." Mrs. Green sweeps an arm across the cluster of us sitting in the cold, blue cushioned seats. "Several of them have already pulled their children out."

"What is she going to do about that?" David whispers. "We've lost like five people just from Cast One alone."

"If anyone with a minor part is willing to take on a second role, please see me," Mrs. Green is still talking. "Also, anyone willing to perform their part on a second night, or even a third, as we are now down two Egeuses, I'd be forever in your debt."

Maizy snorts. "She wants us to memorize more lines? As if."

Raine raises her hand. "Hippolyta's only got a few lines. I could pick up another part, and I could do both the Wednesday and the Friday night performances, but not Thursday."

"Thank you, dear. Now, for the wedding scene in the end, we can place large mirrored panels across the back of the stage to give the effect of having a larger crowd onstage. But honestly, looking at these numbers and given the wishes of the council members, I don't know whether it even makes sense to carry on or not."

"Mirrors onstage?" Starla whispers. "Isn't that like major bad luck?"

"Let's take a vote on it," Colton says, standing up. "Who wants to see this thing through to the end?" He raises his own hand high. David, Starla, Raine, and I raise our hands. As do Lucas, Ferris, Peter, and several others.

Bethany and her friend Alicia are the only two who don't. With a scowl, Bethany finally raises hers and elbows Alicia into going along with it.

"See, Aunt Carol?" Colton says. "We're all in this together, and we've come this far. We can all handle one more week."

Our director begins to clap her manicured hands slowly. "Bravo, my dears. You are all stars in my book. And professionals, too. The show must go on and all that." Tough as she is, she looks a little teary-eyed. "Okay, then, let's get to work. First up on today's schedule is Act Two. I need Oberon, Puck, and Titania ready to go. "Anyone interested in extra parts come see me. I need a Theseus and an Egeus"—she pauses to look through the pages on her clipboard—"and a Peaseblossom and a Moth."

Mrs. Green ascends to the stage as soon as the scene is over to lecture Bottom and the others. "The danger, when you have so many lines that rhyme, is falling into a singsongy rhythm. Don't rap out your lines, Peter. You must be perfectly mindful of what you are saying at all times. And you must make sure your audience understands the sense of what you are saying as well."

"Mrs. Green," Raine asks. "We've been talking about theater superstitions. Is it true you're not supposed to peek out through the curtains during a play?"

She laughs. "I have heard that. But some director or stage manager probably came up with that one to keep the actors from playing with the curtains. It destroys the whole illusion."

"What about not speaking the last line?" Starla asks.

Mrs. Green frowns for a moment. "The last line . . . oh! You're not supposed to say the last line of the play during rehearsals. You must save it for the real performance."

"But why?" Bethany asks.

"I'm not sure." Mrs. Green says. "But Cast One is going to run through the whole thing this afternoon. Everything except the last line."

★ ★ ★

"*Give me your hands, if we be friends, And Robin shall restore amends.*" David forgets at the last minute, and says all of Puck's final piece. Everyone gasps, despite Mrs. Green's promises that it doesn't mean anything. But a chill settles on the back of my neck, and I know that something bad is going to happen before we get to perform this play.

CHAPTER 16

Saturday is a set day, and we have students from SCAD all over the place, directing all three casts in painting and hammering and costume sewing.

Starla and Raine are attending a workshop on making fairy wings, but I have the final fitting for my gown. Dress rehearsal is Tuesday night, and I'm starting to get nervous.

The air smells like burning metal. Some SCAD students have convinced Mrs. Green to let them design the palace in Athens, and they would have turned it into a Japanese Shinto temple if Mrs. Green hadn't put her foot down. She wants a traditional production of this Shakespearean play. Classical Greek costumes and sets for the Athenians, with a more mystical and glittery look for the fairy folk. Thank goodness she's not making us wear green body paint, like in one of the British productions I watched on YouTube. I would not want to be Naked Green Titania.

The seamstress is grimacing at me with pins in her mouth. "Hold still, please."

"Sorry." My tulle skirt itches.

A girl with spiky jet-black hair and a nose ring watches us and doodles on her clipboard. She's in charge of hair and makeup and has been following me around all morning trying to decide what to do with my curls. "Maybe some dreads . . ." she suggests.

"What would Shakespeare say?" I ask, alarmed. "Even more important, what would Mrs. Green say?"

She rolls her eyes. "Right. Mrs. G is so boring."

"Can't I just have a crown of roses?" I ask. I like roses.

"There," the seamstress says, sitting back on her heels and looking up at me. "Your majesty," she adds with a formal wave of her hand.

I turn to look in the mirror. This is the most beautiful dress I've ever seen. It's lavender and delicate and magical. I can't wait to see this costume with my hair done. Hopefully with roses. And not dreadlocks. "Thank you so much!" I say, breathless.

I have to hurry to change back into my human clothes, the ratty UGA T-shirt I wore so I could paint flats. When I come out of the dressing room, Melinda, the seamstress, is waiting for me to hand over the dress.

"Don't let her talk you into the dreads," she tells me, hanging the dress back in the enormous costume closet.

"It was just an idea!" I hear from across the room.

I find Starla and Raine in one of the rehearsal rooms off to the left of the stage. Starla is wielding a glue gun and Raine is modeling a very sparkly pair of wings. Too bad Hippolyta is a mortal lass. She makes a fetching fairy.

"Feeling better today?" she asks.

Thursday was so embarrassing. "I'm fine." My parents wanted me to stay in bed all weekend, but the attic gets too hot during the day. They put a small air conditioner in the tiny window up there, but now I have no view and the attic feels cave-like and I get claustrophobic. I begged them to let me come to the theater today just to get out of the house.

Starla pulls something out of her purse. "Check this out! My ghost hunter friend let me borrow one of his infrared cameras to sweep the theater tonight."

"Tonight?"

"Tell your parents we're pulling an all-nighter. Colton's got the security code for the theater, and we'll convince our aunt we need to stay late to finish the scenery."

I have a hard time believing my mom will let me stay out past midnight, but I shrug. "Sounds like fun."

Raine waits until Starla goes off to show Colton and David the camera before nudging me with her elbow. "She's already asked you-know-who and he says he'll come."

"Who?"

Her smile is sly. "A certain lifeguard who thinks you're hot."

"You've got to be kidding," I say, blushing. "I almost died on him the other day. And not in a glamorous way at all."

"Come on," Raine says. "You know he likes you, right?"

"But him and Starla . . ." I say, and this is the closest I get to admitting how much I care about him. How much it bothers me that she is the Evil Ex who broke his heart.

"Those two are old news." She glances over at Starla, who is now talking to Mrs. Green. Her EMF detector is nowhere to be seen. "Starla has plans for a big acting career and moving to New York as soon as she finishes college. She decided last year that having a steady boyfriend would hold her back. She's only about casual hookups right now."

"Wait a minute. That's why she broke up with him right after his mom died? Because she didn't want his baggage?"

Raine shrugs. "Actually I think she'd already told him she needed space right before his mom died. She told him it was for the best for both of them. That he deserved a girl who would put him first." Raine plays with one of her dreadlocks.

It sounds to me as if Starla couldn't stand that Lucas couldn't put her first. That grieving for his dying mom and trying to hold his own family together cut into time Starla felt he should have been spending with her. But I could just be a bitter seventeen-year-old who's been scarred by her own relationship experiences. So I keep my opinions to myself.

"Anyway, she's sworn off serious relationships until after college," Raine says.

"But one-night flings are okay?"

Raine nods and stares across the theater at Starla, who is now showing her EMF meter to Peter.

Uh-oh.

Starla giggles as Peter reaches for the device and she holds it away from him. "You have to wait for tonight!" she says. We can hear the seductive tinge to her voice all the way over here.

Raine shakes her head. "She can't help it. She flirts with everyone."

"She's just like Colton," I say.

"Exactly. I don't think Colton can help it, either. Come on, let's go rescue Peter."

If Peter needed to be rescued from Starla's clutches, he doesn't seem to realize it. "Oh hey, Raine." And that is the extent of his conversation with her. "Star, do you think we should call *Ghost Hunters* to check out the theater? Maybe we need professionals here."

Starla rolls her eyes. "We don't need them here. Come on, tonight will be epically fun."

I'm surprised she wouldn't jump at the chance to appear on a SyFy program.

I blush when Lucas comes over to talk to Peter about the lighting. I do not look at Raine. Or Starla. If Raine knows of my not-so-tiny crush on Lucas, then certainly Starla sees it, too? Even Colton noticed. And what if Raine is right about him thinking I'm hot?

Of course he thought I was hot. On Thursday I had heat exhaustion. That has to be what she meant.

I feel cold fingers graze the back of my neck and give me a squeeze. I nearly jump out of my skin. "Ready to find your ghost tonight, Natalicious?" Colton asks.

"What do we do if we find her?" I ask him, heart pounding.

Starla's smile is scary. *Though she be but little, she is fierce!* "We'll let the voodoo priestess handle her."

Raine crosses her arms and grins. "I can take on a ghost."

The lights above us blink with a hissing noise.

Raine's eyes get huge as her grin disappears. "Probably."

Everyone else laughs except me. The hair on the back of my neck stands up, and I turn around, expecting to see Colton reaching for me again. But there's no one there.

When Mrs. Green and the other SCAD students leave, there are only seven of us left. Lucas, me, David, Colton, Raine, Peter, and Starla. Lucas has already dropped his sister off at the twins' house to spend the night again.

"Okay, first things first." Starla pulls a bottle of rum out of her purse. "Colton, hit the drink machine."

Our group erupts in loud whoops and woots. David goes with Colton, and the boys come back with armfuls of Cokes.

Lucas is standing beside me, frowning up at the lights. "I should really go check those. I hope there's not a short up there."

"You hope it really was the ghost?" I ask, grinning.

He smiles, too, and it makes my insides turn to jelly. "Only if it's a friendly ghost."

"Like Casper?" I'm suddenly hyperaware that all the others, while still talking and spiking drinks and carrying on, are watching Lucas and me. It makes my head feel weird, and I can't concentrate on what Lucas is actually saying to me.

He's staring at me. "Nat? Are you okay?"

I nod, and suddenly realize how awkward nods are. I don't

know what to do with my hands. Should I hold them at my sides? On my hips? Fold them across my chest? Why have I never thought about this before? And why am I suddenly so concerned with it now? "Totally fine," I lie with a smile.

He's not buying it. "Let's get you something to drink. Alcohol-free." He takes my hand and gives it a tug. I feel five pairs of eyes staring at us. I want to see Starla's reaction, but I'm scared to turn around. Instead, I let Lucas lead me out to the hall where the drink machine is.

"Oh wait, my purse is back there," I say.

"I've got it." He pulls some change out of his pocket and gets me a Diet Dr Pepper.

I want to kiss him for remembering. But of course I don't. Because everyone would know the minute we walk back into the theater. Walking back in is worse. Because now we have to face the gang. But Colton has picked up Starla and is twirling her around over his shoulder. So no one is paying attention to us.

I think everyone's already getting a little buzzed, too. Raine and Peter are getting cuddly. Starla seems to approve. "There she is!" Starla says, pointing to me. "Now we can get this party started. Where's my EMF meter? Where's my effing EMF meter?" She cracks up at her own joke. So does Peter. "Here it is! Nat, come here."

I take a step away from Lucas toward them. Starla waves her ghost-detecting gadget up and down in front of me. "Okay, so you're not a ghost. Just had to check."

I roll my eyes.

"So, I think the best thing to do is to split up," Colton says. Raine giggles. "Star, you and David, come with me, Peter and Raine, go with Lucas and Nat. You guys take the infrared, and we'll take the EMF."

Their group decides to explore the balcony and the lighting booth while we head backstage.

We get as far as the men's dressing rooms when we hear footsteps in the fly above us. Raine squeezes Peter's arm. "It's just the air-conditioning," Lucas says. Although I think he's trying to convince himself as much as the rest of us.

Peter holds the infrared camera up over his head. "Whoa. Check out the cold air."

"Moving through the air-conditioning ducts?" Raine asks. "That's not a ghost."

"I knew that," Peter says. "My uncle uses one of these to check for leaks when he fixes AC units. Still looks pretty cool."

We hear the same noise again overhead.

"That's coming from above the air ducts," Raine says. "Is there a way we can get up there?"

Lucas squints. "I think there's a ladder over behind that curtain." He leads us past the swinging curtains and pushes them aside. The ladder is attached to the cinder-block wall, but the bottom rung is more than six feet off the ground. He looks around. "There," he says to Peter, nodding toward a giant wooden crate over by the curtains. Empty now, it had been the shipping container for the new lighting rigs.

Together they push and shove until the crate is close to the wall. I find another, smaller crate and push that over so they can use it to get up on top of the large crate.

Peter jumps up onto the large crate first, with Lucas following him.

"Y'all can't leave us down here alone," Raine says, her eyes wide.

"We can't all fit up there on the ladder," I point out. I have no desire to go up there. Of course I'd rather not be left alone down here, either.

Peter starts climbing the ladder. "I've got the camera. I'll go up and have a look around and be right back."

Lucas steps down onto the small crate and jumps down.

"It's probably just a rat," Raine says, craning her head to keep an eye on Peter. "Hope it doesn't bite you."

"Shhh!" Peter whispers from above us.

In the silence, I strain to hear any paranormal noises from the rafters.

Instead I hear something bang against the ladder and Peter's "Shit!"

The infrared camera bounces off the crate and lands on the floor in pieces.

"Oh crap," Raine says, going to pick the pieces up. "Star's gonna kill us."

"I don't think there's anything up there anyway," Peter says, jumping down onto the floor.

"Wait a minute. I think it can be put back together," Raine says. "It didn't break. I'll be right back." She takes off down the hallway.

"Wait, where are you going?" I ask.

"I've got a manicure set in my car. I think I can use the cuticle thingy to fix this."

Lucas frowns. "Peter, go with her. She doesn't need to be wandering back here alone."

"He's right. Hang on, Raine." Peter lopes after her.

We can't hear David and the others. I guess they're still up in the balcony. I pull out my phone to text my brother, but I'm not getting a signal. "Seriously?" I say, sighing.

"It's like a bunker back here." Lucas knocks his knuckles against the cinder-block walls. "Want to head back toward the front stage and see if we can find them?"

"Might as well. We don't have any ghost-hunting equipment now."

He doesn't seem to be in a hurry, though.

Neither am I. I lean back against the cool cinder-block wall and look up at Lucas. Now would be the perfect time for him to confess his undying crush on me and swoop me into his arms.

Except that Starla is his ex. And I don't want to be some summer rebound girl.

Lucas's eyes stare into mine, and I suddenly forget about the cold wall behind me. My cheeks feel feverishly warm. Why does he have to be so beautiful? Why does he have to be so broken? He deserves someone who isn't broken, like me. Someone who is strong enough to be there for him when he needs her.

"Natalie," he whispers, moving closer. "You look a little pale."

"I'm fine," I whisper back, my throat dry. Tell him we should probably head back to the others, Natalie. Tell him. Move away from the wall before he comes any closer.

He reaches his hand out, touching my cheek. I can't move. I don't want to move. There is no place on this planet where I'd rather be. I hold my breath.

Lucas is holding his breath, too. I'm afraid he's going to kiss me. I'm afraid he won't. Oh God, why can't I walk away? This is bad.

A hysterical giggle bubbles up out of me. "This is totally out of a horror movie plot. You know? The group gets divided and then separated again and people keep disappearing until there's only one person left. One of us is about to disappear."

Lucas takes half a step back to look at me. But he smiles. "I'm not going anywhere, Nat." He leans back in and his lips press against mine.

My hands instinctively fly up to his chest. Not to push him away, but to hold on. I feel his heart thumping beneath my fingertips.

His hands curve around my waist, pulling me closer. I tug on his shirt, closing the space between us.

I panic and give him a shove. "I can't. This is too dangerous."

"What are you afraid of, Natalie?" His hands squeeze my waist affectionately. "There aren't any ghosts interested in us back here."

"No, it's not that." I pull away from him, fold my arms across my chest. "You and Starla were a thing."

His shy smile falters. "I wanted to tell you, but I really didn't know how to bring it up. It just seems awkward. Especially if you aren't interested in me the way I'm interested in you."

I stare at the design on the front of his shirt, reaching up and tracing my finger over the letters. I'm too shy to keep looking up at his face. "I'm definitely interested," I whisper.

He gathers me against his chest, his lips pressed against the top of my head. "Good to know," he whispers back.

I sigh. "I can't date a friend's ex. It's against the Girls' Code."

"You think she'll mind?" Lucas laughs. But it's not a nice laugh. It's tinged with pain.

Whoa. Now I'm certain he's still hurting from their breakup. He's not over her at all. Get out, Nat. Before he breaks your heart. "Come on, we should go find the others." I push past him and head down the dark hallway. I pull out my phone for light. I can see the red glow of the EXIT sign at the other end of the hall.

"Nat, wait." I hear him behind me, but he's not following me. Good. Now he's the one left alone in the dark. Ha. Horror movie victim number three. And it's not me.

That's really not funny, I tell myself. It's not like there's an ax murderer running amok here. No one's actually getting hurt. They're all just . . . disappearing. I've got to get out of here.

Except, did I just hurt Lucas? Did I piss him off?

I pass the EXIT sign, which only leads to a right turn. I turn and head down the next hallway, looking for another EXIT sign. This place isn't that big. I've walked these hallways several times during the day. With lights. It can't be too hard to navigate in the dark.

Another corner, and no more EXIT signs. Why am I lost? I

turn around and head back the way I came. A left turn and I should be back in the hallway where I left Lucas.

He's not there. He must have taken the other hallway.

"Lucas?"

There's no answer, of course. I want to scream at my idiocy. I follow the hall around the corner, but it's still empty.

"Lucas!"

Of course, he's probably mad that I left him. I was sort of a bitch after that one amazing, heart-exploding kiss.

"Lucas!" I shout and it echoes against the empty, cold concrete walls. There's no other sound back here. I can hear my own breathing, growing ragged and uneven.

I could just sit down here and wait for someone to come looking for me, or I could keep walking in the dark. My phone is losing its charge, of course, and I know I won't have its light for much longer.

I want to scream. I kick the wall instead, not really hard, but enough to make my toes hurt. Effing Lucas.

I hear laughter somewhere. "David?" I shout. I head down the hallway, toward the sound. Maybe my brother has decided to come looking for me.

Instead of the double doors I'm expecting, I run smack into a wall of curtains. Okay, at least I know I've found the back of the stage. "David!" I shout. "Where are you?"

But I push the curtain back only to reveal another curtain. And another and another. I try not to panic as the heavy canvas tangles around me. I must be imagining things, because it feels as if the curtain is tightening around me.

Don't panic, Nat. Take deep breaths.

Do not panic.

CHAPTER 17

*O grim-looked night,
O night with hue so black.*

—*A Midsummer Night's Dream*, act 5

No, I can't stop the panic. I can't stop my heart from revving up, the tears from boiling over down my cheeks. I have no idea what's going on or where I am. Or why I can't get out of here.

I hate this theater. I hate Savannah. I hate Lucas Grant. And I really wish I was back in Athens.

Footsteps approach, but no one answers when I call out. "Who's there?"

I can't even tell if the footsteps belong to a male or a female. Maybe a child? Chills dance across my skin. My stomach twists.

I pull at the curtains, but there only seem to be more and more rows. Where is the effing stage? If I could just get to the stage, I could jump down and run up the aisle to the auditorium doors.

Dust from the swirling curtains is starting to make me sneeze and cough. I shouldn't be struggling so much. This shouldn't be so hard.

How many other teenagers get stuck in a curtain? This is embarrassing. LOCAL GIRL VANISHES IN DIRTY THE-

ATER CURTAINS. POLICE BAFFLED AND FAMILY TOO EMBARRASSED TO MOURN.

Ugh.

The footsteps seem to be running in circles around me. Or I'm too confused to notice. I look up toward the top of the curtains and it makes me dizzy. I look down below. Maybe I could drop to the floor and just crawl out under the curtains.

But they drag on the floor and there's no way for me to see what direction I need to go.

I hear the footsteps again, and this time, I hear a faint, high-pitched laugh. Like a little girl's laugh. Or like a creepy doll's laugh.

I clutch the curtain in terror. Maybe there is a ghost named Lily after all. Has anyone ever been killed by a ghost before? In real life? Not just in a horror movie?

The laughter gets closer and then fades away, then grows closer again and backs away. She's toying with me, whoever she is.

I push at the curtains again, but still can't find the opening.

She laughs at me again.

Frustrated, I sink to the floor and scream. As loud as I can. Even if everyone else is gone, maybe some homeless person in the alley behind the theater will hear me and rescue me.

My throat burns, but I keep screaming. It might keep the ghost away.

The footsteps sound heavier now. Not a child's steps, but someone bigger. "Nat?"

"Natalie!" Raine's voice carries over the others.

"Nat!" David's voice sounds exasperated. I hear the curtains being pulled back and forth. "Where are you?"

"I don't know!"

"Hang on, we're coming."

More curtains get pushed aside, and the footsteps get closer. Human footsteps now. I'm grateful for the sound.

"Dammit, how many curtains are there?" Colton asks.

Someone sneezes.

"Natalie, keep talking to us," Raine says.

"Boo," I say. My throat hurts. I couldn't scream anymore even if I wanted to.

"I think we're almost there."

The metal rings holding the curtains jingle as they tug and pull at the canvas. I just sit still and wait for my rescuers.

"How in the hell did you get these curtains so tangled?" Colton asks.

"I think I had help. From a ghost."

"What?"

With another tug, the curtain gives way, and I see Raine, Starla, David, Colton, and Peter all staring at me. David helps me up.

"I was trying to find my way back to the front, and my phone died. I tried to push the curtains aside, but there were footsteps, and a little girl laughing. She kept running in circles around me, laughing."

My legs are trembling. "Where's Lucas?"

"He went to get Caitlyn," Starla says. "He had a phone call from her, saying she wasn't feeling well. He said he got separated from you back here, so he sent us to find you." She stares at me. "I don't think he knew you were in trouble, or he wouldn't have left."

"Don't be silly. I'm fine," I lie. "Besides, Caitlyn needs him if she's sick."

David looks at me. They're all looking at me.

"I'm fine. Did anyone find anything on the ghost-hunting equipment?"

Colton glances at Starla. She holds her EMF meter out. "Not really. We didn't get anything. And Raine said the infrared camera wasn't working."

"By the time I got it fixed, we realized you were missing and started looking for you."

"Anything popping up now?" But I'm pretty sure there won't be. I can't hear the ghost anymore. She's had her fun and now she's gone to wherever ghosts go when they're not scaring the crap out of people.

"Nope," Colton says, peeking over Raine's shoulder. "It's clean."

Starla's shoulders slump. "Maybe this place isn't haunted after all."

"So you don't think there's a ghost now?" I ask. "No little girl wreaking havoc and terrorizing us?"

"Thomas said we were welcome to use the equipment tonight, but warned me that they'd investigated this place a few years ago and didn't find anything."

"And the story of Lily is actually attached to the old Howell Theater," Peter says, reading a Web site about Haunted Savannah on his phone. "Not this building."

"There's still a chance there's something here," Starla says. "I mean, all theaters should have at least one ghost. Especially since the ghost light burned out."

"But I just got tangled up in my own paranoia and clumsiness," I say. I've never been so embarrassed.

"I think this creepy building makes us all paranoid," Raine says.

"Are you ready to go home?" David asks.

I nod. I don't want to be here anymore. I'm sick of this place.

"We can take her," Raine says. "I need to be getting home, too."

Colton nudges my brother and David frowns. "All right. Will you text me when you get home?"

"I'm fine." Maybe if I say a lie three times, it will become true. "Please don't worry."

As Colton locks up, I follow the girls to Raine's car and climb in the backseat. David waves his phone at me. "Text me," he mouths. I nod.

Raine and Starla both turn around and look at me. "Are you really all right?" Raine asks. "Are you hurt?"

"No, just shaken up a little."

Starla bites her lip. "Nat, did you and Lucas have a fight? He seemed anxious to leave tonight."

I shake my head. "What would we fight about? What did he say?"

I see Raine's eyes in the rearview mirror shift from Starla to me. She's wondering if we did something else besides fight. Which is probably what she was hoping when she and Peter left us alone back there.

"Tell me what happened with you and Peter," I say, leaning forward and grabbing the back of Raine's seat. "Did he try anything?"

Even in the dark car I can see her blushing. I grin. "Raine! Tell us!"

Starla smiles. "Finally! I was beginning to think it was hopeless for you two!"

"Oh. My. God! He's such a good kisser!" Raine squeals as she turns into my neighborhood.

So is Lucas, but I can't say that. For one, Starla already knows. And for another, it's not like I'll get a happily-ever-after like Raine.

Raine pulls up in front of my house. "Don't forget to text your brother. So he doesn't think we kidnapped you."

"Your brother's really a great guy," Starla says.

I shrug. "He can be when he wants to be. But dumbass forgot my phone is dead. Will one of you text him for me?"

"Texting now," Starla says. "With a ransom note. Mwu-ha-ha."

I roll my eyes. "Thanks for the ride. See you Monday?"

"Dress rehearsal! Woot!" Starla says.

It's almost two in the morning, so I try to be as quiet as possible when I unlock the door. I just want to crawl into bed and not think about Lucas's mind-blowing kiss.

I want to not think about the way his fingers felt curving around my waist in the dark.

I definitely do not want to think about the way he looked when I mentioned Starla. How he's still in love with her, despite what he says.

"You're up late."

I startle, as the light flips on in the living room and I see Grandma sitting on the sofa, holding a digital photo frame.

"So are you," I say, once my heart stops pounding. "What are you doing?"

"Couldn't sleep. Just getting home from play practice?"

"We were working on the set. Dress rehearsal is the day after tomorrow, and we were falling behind."

She's staring at the digital photo frame in her hands. Images fade in and out. Old photos of her, Grandpa, Dad. Me and David. Her and Grandpa. Grandma's wedding dress. A pregnant Grandma. Mom and Dad's wedding. Grandpa and his car.

I sit down on the sofa next to her, gently. She doesn't move or say anything. I don't know what to say to her, so I just sit and keep her company. Until she doesn't want company anymore.

There must be over a hundred photos on this frame. It takes forever before it loops around again. And there's Grandma's wedding dress again. Her long red curls peek out from beneath her veil. She's holding blue hydrangeas and lilies of the valley.

"Blue for madness." Her voice is soft. Sad.

When the photograph of Grandpa standing next to his Charger appears, she touches the screen.

"He was so handsome," I say.

She laughs. "That he was."

Her laugh is comforting. Normal-sounding. So I stand up. "I think I'd better get some sleep. Good night, Grandma."

"Sleep tight. Don't let the ghosties bite."

"What?" I spin around to stare at her.

She looks up at me, surprised. "I said sleep tight."

Maybe I'm just overly exhausted and not paying attention. "Oh. Thanks."

"All you all right?"

"I'm fine. Just tired."

"Taking your medication?" she asks.

I glare at her. "Yes. Are you?"

Grandma smiles. And her smile gives me a chill. "Perhaps you should run along to bed, Natalie. Fatigue can be dangerous when you're already emotionally fragile."

I turn and hurry up the stairs to the attic. I had turned the air conditioner off before I left the house this morning, so now my room feels like an oven. I turn the unit on and crank it up to its coldest setting. I am exhausted, but I turn on my laptop to search for Savannah ghost stories. I can't go to sleep until I know for sure. I search for Lily, the five-year-old theater ghost.

And find her. Lily Marcetti. My stomach clenches. The five-year-old daughter of traveling performers from Italy. Died in 1889. Inside the Howell Theater. Not the Savannah Theater, which was originally known as the Fox Theater. The St. Charles Theater downtown is also supposed to have several resident ghosts. But I can find nothing supernatural online about the Savannah Theater.

No ghosts. It was all in my head.

No ghosts at all.

I plug my phone into its charger. I'll have to text David in the morning to make sure he knows I'm okay.

I crawl into bed, hoping I'll fall asleep as soon as my head hits the pillow, but images from this evening tumble over and over in my mind. The curtains that trapped me. Lucas's kiss.

Grandma's wicked smile. Lucas's kiss. Lucas's face when I mentioned Starla. I can't get my mind to shut down. To stop thinking.

Just breathe, Natalie. One of the therapy techniques we learned at Winter Oaks. Which makes me think of Lucas again, but I try to focus on my breathing. In and out. In and out. I count my breaths and try not to think about anything else.

One thing I cannot deny anymore. The ghost has been nothing but a hallucination. I'm really sick in the head after all.

In the morning I will ask Mom to take me to the doctor and see about getting stronger medicine.

CHAPTER 18

Mom calls and the doctor is able to squeeze me in early Monday morning. He's not happy about my trip to the emergency room earlier last week, nor is he happy when I tell him I think I'm hearing voices and seeing ghosts.

At Winter Oaks, the doctors couldn't officially diagnose me with schizophrenia after only one psychotic episode. And since it was drug-induced, there was a small chance I might never have another break again. But given my family history, I can't believe that. I just know that one of these days I'll finally slip into the deep end and wind up like Grandma. I have no doubt of it. Especially when I'm seeing ghosts in the theater.

"I don't know if I want her to continue with the play," Mom says.

"Do you feel threatened? Do you feel as if you're in any danger when you are in the theater?" Dr. Snow asks me.

I shake my head. Not anymore. There never was a ghost. It was just my broken mind all along.

"We've discussed the need for keeping up her social interactions," Dr. Snow is saying to Mom. "I'd like for her to see the play through. It's a challenge that I think she's more than up to meeting." He writes something on his tiny prescription pad and hands it to Mom. "We'll increase her dosage of Zyprexa and see if that helps. You said the dress rehearsal is tonight?"

When I nod, my doctor smiles. "Break a leg, Miss Roman."

"It's just a superstitious saying," Mom says as we're driving back home. "You wish an actor bad luck so the opposite will happen."

I roll my eyes. "I know that."

"Are you sure you're up for tonight?"

My stomach is a mess of angry nerves, but I nod. "I'm sure." I know my lines, I know my blocking. I'm excited about wearing The Dress.

I'm not excited about seeing Lucas.

Grandma shakes her head when she sees my new prescription. I swallow my pills with a swig of Diet Dr Pepper. "They'll just keep upping that dosage until they turn you into a vegetable."

"How do you all feel about Chinese takeout for lunch?" Mom asks, trying to keep the peace.

"Or sushi?" David asks hopefully. "I've heard some good things about that new place on Bull Street."

"Too much mercury in fish," Grandma says. "I'd rather have MSG."

"Nat?" Mom asks for my opinion.

I have to side with Grandma. "Let's do Chinese. I need crabmeat Rangoon for good luck."

David goes and picks up lunch for us, and brings Colton back with him. And a box of sushi.

And no Rangoon. "They were out. Sorry."

But because I was pinning my good luck on that crab Rangoon, I worry that it's a bad omen for tonight. I skip the General Tso's chicken and barely nibble on the lo mein.

Mom and Grandma eat in the kitchen, but we take our food into the living room. David and I sit on the couch, Colton plops down on the floor next to us, his food on the coffee table.

Colton runs lines with me. He seems to be humming with a wild and nervous energy. He is already becoming Oberon. "Sorry I have to drug you tonight, Natalicious."

"Just don't take advantage of me," I say.

David snorts.

"I don't think your beau would be happy with me," Colton says, and ducks before I can stab him with a chopstick.

David frowns. "Nat, did something happen between you and Lucas last night?"

I turn redder than the General Tso's chicken. "No. Why?"

"Oh, I think something did happen," Colton says. "Look at that adorable blush."

"Tell us, Nat," David says, tossing fortune cookies to me and Colton. "What is going on with you two?"

"Nothing. I don't think he's ready to start seeing anyone just yet." I take my cookie out of its wrapper, but don't open it yet.

"So he's a little damaged," Colton says. "Aren't we all? If he wasn't broody and broken, you probably wouldn't want him anyway."

"There's broody and then there's still hung up on your ex," I mutter.

Colton bursts out laughing. "What planet are you living on?" he says. "Lucas? Hung up on Star?"

Surely he knows. Starla is his cousin. "I'm serious. You didn't see the look on his face last night when I asked about them. He still has a broken heart."

Colton stops laughing. "Oh, Natalicious. You can still have a broken heart without having feelings for the person who broke it. Trust me, I know this personally."

David leans over and gives Colton a kiss on the top of his

head. They're totally mad about each other, and as happy as I am for them, I want someone to be that mad about me. Crazy mad in love with me.

"You really think he's over her?" I ask, trying not to sound too hopeful.

"They should have broken up before Mrs. Grant died, but yeah. I think he's over her now." Colton swings one arm around me and one around David. "It's time he gets some happiness. You, too."

Maybe he's right, but I still worry about my impending psychotic break. Mental stability is probably one of the most important qualities Lucas looks for in a girlfriend. If not, it should be.

I ride with David and Colton to the theater. My stomach is in knots and I can't think straight. Maybe Chinese food wasn't the best pre-dress-rehearsal lunch.

Mrs. Green is tapping her feet and points toward backstage. David tugs on my ponytail.

"Break a leg," Colton says, laughing, as they both disappear into the boys' dressing room.

I look up and down the hallway. There's nothing frightening or ominous about it right now. Maybe because I can hear laughter coming from the girls' dressing room.

Human laughter, not creepy ghost giggling.

I push open the door and take a deep breath. It's time to put on THE DRESS.

There are more SCAD students helping out again today. Melinda smiles when she sees me and waves me over. She is going to be my personal dresser.

"Natalicious!" Starla says, stealing Colton's nickname for me. I really don't like it when other people use it. "Are you ready?"

Raine gives me a regal grin. She's already wearing her gold-trimmed toga and is busy adding gold ribbons to her long hair. She's going to make a beautiful Amazon queen.

"I'm ready," I tell Starla, and if I say it enough times, I might convince myself.

Starla's costume for Helena is a bright yellow velvet gown, with golden trim. "I read somewhere that it's unlucky to wear blue onstage," she whispers, nodding toward the other side of the dressing room. Bethany's dress is a royal blue. Starla giggles.

"Should we worry about Bethany?" I ask, as Melinda starts helping me take my clothes off. "Maybe we should say something? So they can find her another costume?"

Raine shrugs her Amazonian shoulders. "Mrs. Green already tried. Bethany said she loves that color and refuses to wear anything else."

"Why is blue unlucky?" I asked. I always thought blue was a lucky color. Not as lucky as purple though. Purple has always been my favorite. Which is why I love Titania's dress so much.

"Probably just because blue was an expensive dye and the theater companies didn't want to waste money on expensive costumes," Starla says.

"Blue is for madness," Melinda says, then points at Starla. "And yellow is the Devil in Disguise."

Starla glares at her, but my dresser doesn't notice. She's too busy helping me with the bodice. I think of Grandma and the blue hydrangeas on her wedding day. Blue for madness, indeed.

"And lavender is for enchanted fairy queens." Raine squeals as I slip the dress on over my head. "Oh my God, you look incredible!"

Melinda tugs on the laces in the back and I have trouble breathing. "Suck it in," she says. "We need to cinch it tight. The headpiece isn't quite done, so you won't be able to wear it until tomorrow night. But I think you're going to like it."

The bodice is cut low in a sweetheart design, edged in silver lace. The long sleeves hang off the shoulder and I'm suddenly nervous about Mom and Dad seeing me in this dress tomorrow night. Especially now that Melinda has squeezed my boobs so I have cleavage. Like, Victoria's Secret cleavage.

I pull the ponytail holder out of my hair and my curls are set free. I stare at myself in the mirror.

And I don't even recognize myself. I see Faerie Queen Titania staring back at me. It gives me chills.

Or that could just be because my shoulders are naked.

We hear Mrs. Green's voice in the back hallway. "Five minutes, minions! I want to see all cast members in the green room in five minutes!" Her high heels click down the hallway.

"Are you two ready?" Raine asks. Starla is still arranging her hair. Her aunt made her get rid of the blue and purple streaks for the play. Starla didn't want her blond to clash with the dress, so now she has hair as black as Colton's. It's jarring to look at her. It gives her a Snow-White-stole-Belle's-dress look. Sort of.

Raine pushes the door open and hurries us out. "Let's go break some legs."

I follow the girls into the green room, where most of the cast is already assembled. "Plenty of room in here, make room. Make room," Mrs. Green says. She sweeps a sharp glance across the crowd, and smiles. A rare and precious Mrs. Green smile. "I know you've all been busting your ass these last few days, and stepped up more than I could have possibly hoped. I just want you all to know how very proud I am of you."

Our fearless director makes us stand in a circle and hold hands. I reach for Raine's hand on the right side, and look over to see who is standing on my left.

Lucas. He's staring at me, his eyes open wide in wonder.

I grab his hand, since he's not offering it.

Something electric passes from his fingers to mine, and I

know he feels it the same instant I do. I hear his sharp intake of breath. He squeezes my fingers, gently. My whole body sings and I can't focus on anything Mrs. Green is saying.

Lucas leans his head toward me. I can smell basil and soap on him. He must have been working at Giorgio's this afternoon. "You look beautiful," he whispers.

We're all supposed to be quiet and focus on getting into character. But I forget all about Titania. My head is full of Lucas. Not Demetrius, even though he makes a very fine Athenian lord indeed. He looks like Hercules, with leather armor fitted over his white toga, and a crimson cape slung over his shoulder.

"Everyone close your eyes and take a deep breath," Mrs. Green says. I close my eyes, but all I think about is Lucas, with his bare, muscular arms standing very near to me and my bare shoulders. I can feel the heat radiating off of him. Somehow, I don't feel so cold anymore.

Lucas's thumb grazes the edge of my wrist, ever so slightly. I don't even know if he did it on purpose. But it drives me crazy.

Mrs. Green's voice cuts into my lustful thoughts. "Focus, people. I want you to forget about everything else except your character. Search deep within and explore your physical reactions to your emotions. This is what you must bring to your character to bring her to life."

"So, in her blue gown, is Bethany going to go mad?" I ask as we wait behind the curtains.

"It'll be fun to watch. Tonight should be very interesting," Starla says, pushing us toward the stage. Only she pushes just a little too hard, and I stumble out onto the stage.

Mrs. Green, who is standing center stage, turns and looks at me. "'Twas the fairies that tripped you. Kiss the hem of your dress, Natalie, to appease them."

"Fairies or evil ghosts?" Raine murmurs.

"'Twas Starla that pushed me too hard," I mutter, lifting my skirt and exposing my tulle underskirt to everyone onstage. That gets a few catcalls. I blush as I give the hem a quick kiss and drop the skirt back down. "Ick. This costume is dusty."

Raine and Starla can't help but laugh at me.

Colton has taken on the role of Theseus, too, since Michael dropped out. Mrs. Green told us that in some productions, the actors who play Theseus and Hippolyta also play the roles of Oberon and Titania, as they are "mirrored" roles. The fairies are the dream world versions of the Athenian characters.

And what is really funny to me is the fact that in Shakespeare's time, all the roles were played by male actors, so it must have really been a hoot to watch. Especially to see a guy play Titania, the faerie queen.

Cast Two Titania has dropped out, so Mrs. Green has talked me into performing two nights in a row. It means I will get to wear THE DRESS two more times after tonight.

Some parents have pulled the little kids out, too, the ones that were playing the minor fairies like Peaseblossom and Moth. I think even Mrs. Green was glad to see Hailey and Bailey drop out, though. Those were the most evil five-year-olds I've ever met. Hailey liked to stick her boogers on the arm rests of the theater seats, and Bailey got melted M&M's all over my script. Caitlyn is much better behaved, even if she is a little obsessed with fairies.

Melinda, the costume manager from SCAD and diehard Lord of the Rings fan, and Diana, the ticket mistress, have been appointed backup fairies. Which was probably Melinda's Evil Scheme all along. She was dying for a chance to wear pointy ears and glitter.

The play begins with Theseus and the Athenians, then the Mechanicals come onstage to plot their wedding entertainment. Nerves dance inside my stomach as I wait for my first scene.

I stand at the edge of the curtains with my fairy entourage, waiting for our cue. Colton is waiting on the other side of the stage and he winks, trying to make me smile.

Caitlyn is standing next to me, enraptured by the story coming to life on stage. Finally, David is out there, as Puck talking with one of the pointy-eared fairies. He stumbles over his lines, and I frown. Are we already off to a bad start tonight?

I am Titania, queen of the fairies, I tell myself. And when Puck says, *"But, room, fairy! here comes Oberon,"* and Melinda says, *"And here my mistress. Would that he were gone,"* it's time for me to take the stage.

I say all my lines perfectly, but I almost fall out of the giant bird's nest that Bottom and I are supposed to sleep in.

Lysander drops his sword with a loud *clang* and some of the fairies get lost backstage. All in all, though, we do rather well.

Until Peter gets his head stuck in the giant donkey head. He panics and stumbles into one of the flats, knocking over half of the set.

Mrs. Green closes her eyes and throws her clipboard on the ground. "Stop!" she shouts. "Enough. Everyone out of their costumes and back out here in your seats in twenty minutes."

We scramble to the dressing rooms, where SCAD volunteers are waiting to help us undress. "I think it went well," Starla says. "Bad dress rehearsals mean perfect opening nights."

"Then our opening night should be spectacular," Raine says. "Because tonight sucked spectacularly."

"No lighting disasters," I say. "No injuries. Except Peter's hair. And at least David didn't say the last line of the play again."

Raine frowns. "Peter shouldn't have used so much hair gel."

We hurry back out front to join the boys. Lucas is sitting between Caitlyn and Peter. Disappointed a little, I sit next to Raine on the end.

★ ★ ★

Mrs. Green paces back and forth across the stage, her pointy black heels clicking across the wood. "We're making progress, but I still see contemporary teenagers on this stage. I do not see Shakespearean characters. These characters are not coming alive for me up here. You need to work on this some more." It was time for another of her drama lessons. "To become one with your character, you must find an emotion that you share in common with your character."

Raine and Peter look like they're falling asleep. Only the kids in front are paying attention to our Fearless Director. Not even Starla, whose lifelong ambition is to make it to Broadway.

My phone lights up even though it's on silent. I peek at my screen and grin. Andria has answered my text and says she and Trista are coming to town for the play this weekend. I can't wait to see them again.

"This is tonight's homework for everyone. Think about your character and create an emotional memory for this character using your own emotional memories. Tomorrow night, I want to see real acting up here—not just a bunch of children reciting lines."

We stay after rehearsal to write our emotional memories. David and Colton walk out together. Lucas leaves to take Caitlyn home without saying a word to me.

He must be mad at me for pushing him away last night backstage. But I'm so scared of falling in love with the wrong boy again. And I'm pretty sure he's the wrong boy for me. I'm fairly certain I'm the wrong girl for him.

In the parking lot after, sure that Mrs. Green has left, Starla takes a bottle of vodka out of her backpack.

"What do you think you're doing?" I ask.

She pours some into my can of Dr Pepper. "There, now try it."

Raine holds out her can of Coke. "Libations to appease the theater spirits. I'm down with that."

Starla grins. "Girl, great minds think alike." She adds some vodka to her own Diet Coke, then holds the can up like a toast. "To the spirits in this theater."

"But there aren't any spirits," I say. And I really don't see how getting drunk would appease them if there were.

I know I shouldn't be drinking. But it seems like every time I hang out with these two girls, I end up doing something I shouldn't.

"What a way to get in touch with our emotions," Raine giggles. "I feel . . . happy."

"Me, too," I say. My body seems to be composed of words and poetry. My structure forms from syllables, each muscle and bone stressed or unstressed. The rhythm of iambic pentameter pulses my blood through my veins. My breath, the alliteration of vowels. My body does not look how I feel. I feel drunk on Shakespeare.

At least I try to blame it on Shakespeare. But of course it's just the vodka.

CHAPTER 19

I wake up to my phone chirping, and my head exploding with pain. How much vodka did I drink last night? I remember stumbling into the house before midnight, and crawling up the stairs so I wouldn't make too much noise.

Did I wake anyone up? I remember a light coming on in Grandma's room, but I don't remember talking to her.

Ugh. Every time my phone rings it pierces my eardrums. I try to grab it from my nightstand, but it falls on the floor. Leaning over the side of the bed to pick it up is not a good idea. My head swims and I think I'm going to be sick.

It's Lucas's number. Now I know I'm going to be sick. "Hello?"

"Nat, thank God. Can you do me a really huge favor? Can you watch Caitlyn this morning? I know this is short notice, but I have to be at the pool at nine thirty, and Raine has her first drill team practice at ten. She didn't tell me about it until just now."

That's not my fault. And I don't want to see or speak to Lucas right now. But I can't let Caitlyn suffer because things are weird and awkward between her brother and me. I look at my clock. 8:45.

"Just give me some time to take a shower." And drink some coffee. And become human again. I close my eyes.

"All right. Want me to bring her over to your house or do you want to come over here?"

I don't have a car, but I'm curious about the place where Lucas and Caitlyn live. I'm curious about his father. "I'll come over there," I say. If I hurry, maybe my dad can take me on his way to the hospital.

"It's nice to see you finding new babysitting jobs," Dad says as we head to Lucas's neighborhood. "I'm glad you're getting used to living here."

I shrug. "Savannah's pretty. And I have made a few new friends."

"Do you think your mom likes it here?" he asks.

I really don't. But I don't want to hurt Dad's feelings. "She thinks it's pretty, too. I think once she gets to open her own café again she'll be happier."

Dad frowns. "I wish there was a way for that to happen. But Mom needs to watch Grandma right now."

I don't want to argue with him. "I don't think Grandma likes having a babysitter all the time."

"It doesn't matter what she likes," he says, sighing. "We have to keep her safe. Is this the turn?" he asks.

"Yes." Lucas's house is right next door to Starla's, and I wonder why he didn't ask her to babysit. Seems that it would be so easy for him to turn to her in emergencies. Better her than someone who is crazy.

"All right. Will this family bring you home when you're done?" Dad asks. "I'm going to try to make it home from work in time for the play tonight, but I can't make any promises. Trauma has been crazy these past few weeks."

"It's all right. I understand," I say, opening the door. I can go next door and get Starla to bring me home if necessary. Or I could call David.

Dad reaches over and squeezes my shoulder. "Natalie, break a leg tonight."

I roll my eyes. And it makes my headache come back. "Thanks."

Lucas opens the front door for me. He's wearing his lifeguard uniform and God help me it looks even better than his Hercules/Demetrius costume. He waves to my dad, who's already backing out of the driveway.

"Thanks again. You don't know how much I appreciate this. Cait is bouncing off the walls excited about tonight. You have your work cut out for you."

"Great." I should have taken Motrin before I left home, but I didn't have time.

"Are you okay?" he asks.

"I'm fine. Just nervous about tonight myself."

Lucas cups my face with his hand, strokes my cheek with his thumb. "Don't be. You'll be perfect tonight."

Why does he act like he can't stand to be around me, and then the next minute act like he can't keep his hands off me? I'm tired of being confused.

I put my hand over his. And I think he's going to pull me closer and maybe even kiss me, but we hear someone come out of the house next door. "Lucas? Do you have time to look at my computer before work? I think it might have gotten a virus." Starla's brother, Chance, comes loping across the yard. "Starla and her friend Ferris were using it to watch videos last night."

With a frustrated sigh, Lucas drops his hand away from me and steps back. "Sure."

"Anything I should know before you leave?" I ask. Like, why Ferris was over at Starla's when he's dating Maizy.

"Cait can tell you where everything is. Help yourself to

any food you see. My father stays in his bedroom, but if he does happen to come out, don't be alarmed." He smiles sadly. "He's harmless. I'll be back by four, and then I can take you home. Unless you want to ride with us to the theater."

Chance is looking bored, so I don't keep Lucas any longer. "That's fine," I say. "Have a good day."

He turns to follow Chance and I go inside the Grants' home. It's got a similar layout to Starla's house, with an open living room-dining area and the kitchen to the back.

Cait jumps off the couch and runs over to give me a hug. "I'm so glad you're here. Want to watch cartoons? Or play with Rufus? We can be fairies all day today!"

"But I didn't bring my wings!" I say.

"I've got an extra pair you can borrow."

We have a fairy tea party in her room, which consists of wearing glitter-covered wings and eating Little Debbie snack cakes with orange juice. I let Caitlyn be the fairy queen. I'm just a lowly fairy princess.

Lucas texts me on his break. *Everything going okay?*

Yes. Stole some Motrin from your bathroom for a headache. Hope it's okay.

That's fine. Sorry if Caitlyn gave you a headache.

"Who are you texting?" Caitlyn asks, plopping down on the couch with me. "Is it Lucas?"

It's not her fault. Woke up with one. Motrin and the fairy cakes made it go away.

"Tell him to bring us some pizza!"

"He's not at the pizza shop today, he's at the pool."

"But I want pizza for lunch."

"I don't think he'd be home in time for lunch anyway. Do you have any frozen pizza we could make?"

"Lucas never buys frozen pizzas. He gets sick of pizza sometimes." She sounds sad.

"Let's see what you do have in your kitchen. I'm sure there's something we can make that would be a proper fairy queen's lunch." I remember Lucas mentioning her love of macaroni and cheese with cinnamon and repress a shudder.

"Okay!"

But I'm startled to find an older man in a bathrobe and Star Wars pajama pants standing in the Grants' kitchen.

"Hey Dad," Caitlyn says. "We're going to make a fairy lunch."

He looks up at me and stares. I'm not sure what he's thinking, so I give a little wave. "Hi, I'm Natalie. Lucas asked me to babysit this morning."

"Excellent." Mr. Grant nods and takes his coffee to his room.

He reminds me of Grandma. Raine thinks he's still grieving the loss of Mrs. Grant, but he looks to me like he's far beyond mere grieving. Like he doesn't know how to start living again. My heart breaks for all of them. Cait doesn't seem to be upset by his behavior.

"Come on. I bet we have some leftover lasagna in here." She opens the refrigerator.

"Do fairies eat lasagna?" I ask her. My phone beeps again.

It's from Andria. *On our way to Savannah! Excited about tonight?*

Of course! I text back. *Want to get something to eat after the play?*

Always ready to eat. You pick the place and we will treat you. Heading back on the road. TTYL!

Caitlyn sets a container of mushrooms on the counter, along with a loaf of bread, some Lucky Charms cereal, and a jar of mayonnaise. My hangover suddenly returns.

"We'll use the Lucky Charms as magic sprinkles, and we can make magic mushroom sandwiches."

I grab a handful of cereal out of the box, eating the marshmallows first. "Maybe we should just eat the lasagna."

I convince her to put away the mayo and mushrooms, and after a huge bowl of reheated lasagna, Caitlyn is ready for a nap. "Will you come take a nap with me?" she asks.

"Sure, all fairies need their beauty rest," I say. I plan to only lie down on the bed with her until she falls asleep, but I'm more tired than I thought I was.

I wake up to find Lucas standing over Cait's bed.

I jump up, terrified that she's woken up and run off, that she's been doing something dangerous like juggling knives in the kitchen. But she's still sleeping next to me, snoring like an old man.

Lucas smiles, sinking down on the mattress next to me. My skin heats up, all of my molecules aware of just how close he is. "Um, I don't think a twin bed is built for three people," I whisper. "Or even two and a half."

He blushes. "I'd tell you my bed is bigger, but that sounds like a proposition, doesn't it?" His voice is low, barely above a whisper to avoid waking his sister, but it makes my skin tingle.

My blush outblushes his. I do not need to think about Lucas and his bed right now. "Is it four already? Should I wake Caitlyn up to get her ready to go?"

"I got off work early. You can sleep a little longer if you'd like."

I'm wide awake now. There's no way I could fall back asleep. "Did you eat? Want me to make you something?"

"I'm fine." He smiles and it breaks my heart. Why does he look so happy, so peaceful? We have to be onstage in front of a million people in just a few hours. The panicky butterflies come back. He sees me frown and his smile fades. "Hey, what's wrong?"

I try to take a deep breath, because I know that's the first thing he'd tell me to do. "Tonight, we're going to be out there in front of all those people. What if I forget my lines?"

"Take a deep breath," he says. And I don't bother to point out that I already did. I just take another, and another.

"But don't hyperventilate," he says. "You know your lines. You're not going to forget them."

I stare at him and try to think of my first line. My cue is Puck's conversation with the fairy. And I come on stage with Oberon and he says . . . something . . . and I say . . . oh my God, what do I say? My mouth goes dry. "I already forgot!"

"Close your eyes. You haven't forgotten. Those lines are still in your head."

I close my eyes, but the lines aren't there. I do, however, notice Lucas's hands rubbing up and down my bare arms. How does he expect me to remember anything when he's touching me?

I lean my head against his chest and he wraps his arms around me. "You can do this," he murmurs into my hair. "Come on. Oberon sees you onstage and what does he say?"

His fingers move up and down my back, around my waist. Right now I don't even want to think about the stupid play anymore. My hands slide up his back to hold on to him and I hear Lucas's heart start to race.

"Natalie." His lips are pressed against my forehead now. If I tipped my head back to look up at him, would he kiss me? It's not even something I should be contemplating. We're standing in his baby sister's bedroom, for crying out loud. With his sister sleeping right in front of us.

I wonder if I should remind him what he said about his own bed a few minutes ago.

"Remember what Oberon says?" he asks again, coaxing me to remember. "*Ill met by moonlight . . .*"

"*Ill met by moonlight, proud Titania,*" Caitlyn says, sitting up suddenly.

Lucas doesn't let go of me. But I feel his chest shake, as he tries hard not to laugh. "Does that help?" he whispers.

"*What, jealous Oberon! Fairies, skip hence: I have forsworn his bed and company.*" I pull back to grin at his sister. "Thank you, Caitlyn!" I look up at Lucas. "And you. You have a pretty amazing memory technique there."

He lets go of me with another adorable blush. "I guess I should go jump in the shower. I'm sure I smell like sweat and chlorine."

He smells like Lucas. And I don't care that his five-year-old sister is sitting here watching us. I stretch up on my tiptoes and kiss him on the cheek.

"Eew!" Caitlyn shouts as Lucas grabs me and kisses me back, on the lips. It's just a quick kiss, light and friendly like mine, but there's a promise of better things to come later.

He winks at his sister. I sit back down on the bed, dazed as he leaves to get ready.

"He kissed you!" Caitlyn sings. "Are you his girlfriend now?"

"I don't know," I say, hoping and praying that he can't hear us. "Is that how it works? Does kissing make you boyfriend and girlfriend?"

She rolls her eyes. Hazel eyes just like her brother's. "Haven't you ever had a boyfriend before?"

I don't want to think about any of my past boyfriends. "Have you?" I counter.

"Duh. I had two boyfriends last year."

"And you kissed both of them?" I ask. I wonder if Lucas knows about this.

"Well, I kissed Trey, but Max kissed me." She looks at my glittery toenails. "I wish my toes sparkled like yours."

"Next time I come over, I'll bring sparkly nail polish and paint your toes," I promise.

But Caitlyn finds other topics to chatter about in the car on the way to the theater. Lucas holds my hand while he drives, just like a real boyfriend, but lets go when he pulls into the parking lot. I guess he doesn't want anyone else to know just yet. It makes me sad, but maybe he's right. We need to keep our hands off each other until after the play.

He hasn't mentioned anything about the Midsummer Night's Ball that will take place after our final performance on Saturday. Raine has finally convinced or coerced Peter into asking her, but Starla has been mysteriously quiet about her date. Raine says she thinks it's the guy from the pool, Hunter. Or a SCAD upperclassman. Either one is really too old for her, I think. My mom would lock me in my attic bedroom if I tried to date someone who was legally old enough to drink.

Caitlyn hops out of the back seat and doesn't wait for us to get out of the car. Lucas looks over at me. "Are you ready?"

I nod, taking a deep breath. I'm okay now. Truly. "Thanks."

He looks past me out the car window and nods. "Looks like you have a fan club already."

I open the door, excited that Andria and Trista have made it to town so fast. I didn't think I'd get to see them before curtain. I hop out of the car, but before I take two steps, I stop, because it's not Andria or Trista.

"Hey pretty girl."

Caleb. In Savannah. In the flesh.

"What are you doing here?"

"I came to see the show." He smiles and holds his arms out. "Hug?"

"Introduce us?" Lucas says, getting out of the car and coming around to stand next to me.

Oh, this cannot be happening. Just when I think I'm centered and focused and breathing in and out like an expert zen master, my own Evil Ex has to pop back up in my life.

"Caleb Watters," he says with a smile, holding his hand out to Lucas. "Natalie and I go way back."

Lucas is nice and shakes Caleb's hand. I hold my breath, letting Lucas give his own introduction. "Lucas Grant."

And feel a twinge of disappointment. I tell myself it's not

that I wanted him to declare himself my boyfriend and protector. Because I don't need anyone to protect me from Caleb. But I grab Lucas's arm. "Well, hope you enjoy the show. Come on, Lucas, we have to get ready." I try to pull him toward the front doors of the theater, but he resists.

Why does he want to stay here?

"So you're the one who broke Natalie's heart," Lucas says.

What? How does Lucas know? "He didn't really . . ."

Caleb has the nerve to look sad. "The heart breaking went both ways."

All right, if I have to talk to him now, I might as well get this over. "I told you I didn't want to speak to you again. If it weren't for you, I wouldn't have ended up at Winter Oaks."

Caleb folds his muscular arms against his chest. God, how I used to love his tattoos. "I have a lot to apologize for, Nat. And I know you can't forgive me right now. But I want you to know that I do regret hurting you."

"Well? *Can* you forgive him?" Lucas asks me.

I hate being put on the spot. I can't deal with this right now. I shake my head, still staring at Caleb.

Lucas sighs. "All right. You don't really have time to settle this before the play starts. I think we need to go on inside."

"Before Mrs. Green comes out after us," I say, agreeing. "Goodbye, Caleb." I drag Lucas across the parking lot without looking back.

But Lucas stops me once we get inside. He stares at me, as if searching my face for something. "If you're not ready to forgive him, you're not ready to move on." He leans down and kisses me on the forehead. "Break a leg tonight."

Wait a minute. Wait just a freaking minute. "And what makes you an expert about moving on?" The words fly out of my mouth before I can stop them.

He frowns.

We're standing in the lobby and I'm certain he didn't want to cause a scene in front of the entire cast and crew. Neither do I. I grab his arm and pull him up the stairs to the balcony. "Have you forgiven Starla?" I ask him. "Can you honestly tell me you have no more feelings for her?"

Lucas stares down into the empty seats below. He opens his mouth to say something, but sighs instead.

Now that I've asked him, I'm not sure if I want to know the answer anymore. This is so not an appropriate time to be having this conversation. I'm supposed to be getting into my costume right now. Into my character.

Lucas looks back over at me. "I was about to say that you don't understand, that I had to start getting over Starla while I was at Winter Oaks. But that's stupid. Because you had to do the same thing, didn't you?" He slumps down in one of the seats.

Except I didn't try to kill myself over Caleb. And I realize I'm still not certain what happened to Lucas before he was admitted. I reach out and pick up his hand. "Were you really trying to kill yourself because of her?"

He squeezes my hand, pulling me down onto his lap. He lets out a heavy breath that tickles the side of my neck. "I honestly don't know, Nat. I told everyone it was an accident. My dad, the doctors, my friends. I drank because everyone else did. And everyone else still does. I wanted to fit in. Pretend that nothing ever bothered me. Not Mom dying. Not Dad shutting down. Not Caitlyn crying herself to sleep every night."

Lucas still hasn't let go of my hand, and now he caresses my wrist with his thumb. It's hard for me to concentrate on what he's telling me.

"Starla and I had started growing apart months before my mom got sick. I think we both wanted to move on, but she felt guilty about abandoning me when my family was falling apart. I think it would have been better if she'd just broken up and moved on. But I caught her sleeping with one of the guys that works at the comic book store next to the Pirate House."

I put my free hand on Lucas's shoulder. "I'm so sorry."

"I guess it just hurt my pride more than anything else. And so I was trying my damnedest not to let anyone know. I drank more than anyone else that night, and came home with a raging headache. I found Mom's bottle of painkillers in the bathroom and decided it would be a brilliant idea to swallow a few of them."

I lay my cheek against Lucas' shoulder and his free hand slides around my waist.

"I'm so sorry, Nat. I have no business asking anything from you. I shouldn't have acted like a dick in front of Caleb. I'm pretty sure he doesn't deserve you, but I don't deserve you either."

He gently picks me up and sets me on the floor. I can't tell for sure, but I think his eyes are watery. Just like mine.

"Come on. We're going to get in trouble if we don't get in our costumes."

Right. Because that's why we're here. There's a show that must go on, and all that.

Lucas hurries ahead of me down the stairs, disappearing into the men's dressing room as if he's never going to see me again. Why does it feel like he's just broken up with me before we even started going out?

I head inside the women's dressing room to put on THE DRESS again. Somehow it doesn't seem quite as magical. Even when the SCAD students fix my hair with a crown of lavender flowers and silver ribbons. Someone sits me down in a chair and does my makeup, painting my face and bare shoulders with glitter.

"Who was that hot blond out in the parking lot?" Starla asks. "And why did Lucas take such a strong dislike to him? Raine shakes her head and grins. "Three guesses why Lucas didn't like him."

If I tell them about Caleb now, I'm afraid I'll start crying. "Long story," I say. "I promise I'll tell you after the play."

CHAPTER 20

Act Three ends and the curtains draw together. My heart thumps so hard, I know even the people in the balcony can hear it. The adrenaline rush is like nothing I've ever felt before. Ten times better than ecstasy.

It's nothing like I expected. The feeling's addictive. No wonder Starla would sell her soul for the acting life. My blood is humming. My breathing hard and fast. I feel more alive than I ever have before. Colton squeezes my hand as the curtains draw back again for the cast to bow. His hand is warm. He bends close to whisper in my ear, "You feel the magic, don't you? Isn't this wild?"

For some strange reason, it seems the fairies and the theater gods and any ghosts haunting the old theater all decided to look upon us with favor and our performance is a success. Mrs. Green beams radiantly as she stands backstage applauding while we take our final bows.

I've remembered my lines. I've remembered my blocking. No one has messed up tonight. We have managed to create the illusion that instead of mere Georgian teenagers, lovelorn Greeks and fairies have inhabited the stage.

I stand between David and Colton just like we've practiced, the roar of applause thundering in my ears. Between bows, I spot my mother and grandmother in the audience, but don't see Andria or anyone else from Athens. The curtain finally closes and everyone starts hugging. We're all sweaty, but no one minds. I see Ferris clap Lucas on the back, on the other side of the crowd. Lucas looks at me and smiles, but doesn't make any attempt to come closer.

I get attacked by a very sparkly Caitlyn. "This was the best night of my entire life!" she shouts. "I'm moving to Broadway when I grow up!"

"Let's move in together!" I say, high on the adrenaline, too. Maybe being an actor wouldn't be so bad after all.

Someone delivers an enormous bouquet of roses to Starla. She squeals when she reads the card, but tucks it away before anyone else can see.

Raine and I get roses, too; hers are from her parents. Mine are from Caleb. I throw them in the trash can on my way to the dressing room.

I push the door open and the goth SCAD student that wanted me to wear dreads helps me out of my costume. "You rocked tonight," she says, carefully removing the accessories from my hair and putting them in a box for tomorrow's show. "Are you planning to attend SCAD when you graduate?"

I nod. I really want to study theater now. "Costume design," I say, smiling shyly at her. "Not acting."

"But you're such a great actress," she says, twisting my hair up in a loose knot so I can finish getting undressed.

Raine and Starla and Bethany enter, giggling. "You didn't wait for the pictures!" Starla said. "My aunt was looking all over for you!"

"Guys, we were all so awesome!" Bethany says, high on post-performance adrenaline. Tonight we're all best friends. "Who's going to IHOP?"

"Nat, some girls out there were looking for you. Are they your friends from your old school?"

"Where were they?" I ask, as I finish pulling on my jeans and a T-shirt. I hang my dress up so Melinda won't yell at me. Maybe Andria and Tris will want to go to IHOP with everyone else. Of course it will be hard to catch up with them with all my new friends around. But I really don't want to risk having to talk about Caleb tonight.

"That blond guy isn't still out there, is he?" I ask.

"Didn't see him," Starla says. "Are you going to tell us about him now, or do we have to bribe you with pancakes?"

I smile, because I know how to stall. "A stack of chocolate chip pancakes with whipped cream. I need to go touch base with my parents and let them know we're going out."

I leave them to finish getting undressed and go searching for Mom or Dad. David finds me first. "Hey, Andria was here, looking for you."

"Where did she go?"

He crosses his arms and frowns. "Caleb was with them. Did you invite him too?"

"Of course I didn't! One of them must have told him about the play. I hadn't even told him what city we moved to."

"Is he trying to cause trouble?" David asks. "Need me to kick his ass for you?"

"Not yet. But thanks for the offer," I say, giving him a hug.

He's surprised, but hugs me back. "Always happy to look out for you, Hippie."

"There she is!" Mom's voice rises above all the other noise around us. I pull away from David and get caught up in her arms. "Dad's so sorry that he couldn't make it. But we're both so proud of you, honey! We all are!"

Grandma is standing behind her. Grandma looks very uncomfortable, amidst all the noise and confusion. But I'm happy she made the trip out of the house. "I'm so glad you guys could make it. But you don't have to stay. I was going to ask if it's all right if I go to IHOP with the rest of the cast."

Mom pulls out her wallet. "Sure. Do you need some money?"

"It would help," I admit. I have got to start looking for a job next week, as soon as the play is over.

"David, you'll bring her home?" Mom asks, still smiling at both of us. "I can't believe how talented my children are!"

"You do make a beautiful Puck," Grandma says to David. He blushes and she grins. "Natalie, you were quite amazing too."

"Thanks." I know not to hug her, that she doesn't like us touching her, so I just smile.

She smiles back. But there's an odd gleam in her eye. Not malicious, but it looks like she is plotting something. Mom needs to get her home quick. I hug Mom again and thank them both for coming. I offer to walk them to their car, but we hear shrieking and giggling behind us as Andria and Trista find me.

"NATALIE!" they both scream.

David ends up walking Mom and Grandma out so I can hug my friends.

"I can't believe you really drove all the way here!" I say, jumping up and down with them. "How was the drive?"

"Not bad," Andria says. "We stopped at every Dunkin Donuts between Athens and here."

"I guess you're not hungry for pancakes then," I say. "The cast is going to IHOP to celebrate and I was hoping y'all would come, too."

Trista glances around. "That depends. Are you going to introduce us to some of your hot actor friends?"

"What about Hank?" I ask her. "And Alex?" I ask, mentioning Caleb's bandmates.

"She's just kidding!" Andria says. "They're out in the car waiting for us. Alex drove, of course!"

Of course. Andria still can't drive, because she had a seizure in April. I am so happy to hear that Andria and Alex are still together, and Hank and Trista too. But it makes me think of Caleb, how we used to think we'd all be dating the boys of Calcifer together and now I've broken up our group.

No, that's not right, I think, staring at these two deliriously happy girls. I'm just not a part of their group anymore. "Did Caleb come with you?" I ask.

Andria's smile fades quickly.

Trista shakes her head. "Effing Hank. I told him not to say a word to that rat bastard."

"Well, he must have said something." I sigh. "Caleb showed up in the parking lot this afternoon."

"Oh my God," Andria said. "Did he behave? When we saw him tonight we told him to go back home."

I guess it could have been worse, but if it weren't for Caleb, I'd probably be introducing Lucas as my new boyfriend right now. I glance around. I haven't seen Lucas in a while. I don't know if he's going to IHOP or not.

Starla and Raine walk over with Bethany. "Are they coming with us?" Raine asks. "We're about to head out."

I introduce everyone quickly and Raine quickly convinces Andria and Tris to bring the boys to IHOP. I decide to ride with them, so I squeeze in the backseat with Tris and Hank.

"Hey, Nat—ouch, what's that for?" Hank says, rubbing his arm where I punch him.

"That is for telling Caleb where I live."

Trista reaches around me and punches him again. "Ouch!" he shouts again.

"And that's for not listening to me, Asshole."

Alex turns around and smiles at me. "How's it going?"

"God, I've missed you all so much," I say, blinking back tears. I miss my old life.

Andria follows Starla's car to the IHOP, while I tell everyone about my new friends. And David's new friends.

"Did he ever come out to your parents?" Trista asks.

I shake my head. "No, but Grandma knows, and I'm scared to death she's going to out him any day now. You'll meet Colton tonight. He and David are perfect for each other."

"And what about you?" Hank asks. "You must have moved on if you weren't happy to see Caleb today."

I frown. "Just because I don't want to be with him anymore doesn't mean there's someone else."

Andria and Trista exchange glances in the rearview mirror. "Oh, there's definitely someone else," Tris says. "Are we going to meet Mr. Someone Else tonight?"

I cover my face with my hands. I'm blushing and I don't even know why.

"Y'all leave her alone," Alex says, grinning. "Maybe David will give us the details."

And maybe Mom gave me enough money to buy my brother's silence. We pull into IHOP and I'm actually relieved to see Lucas's car missing.

No really. It makes this easier.

David is getting out of his truck and says hi to Alex and Hank. He introduces them to Colton and we all go inside.

The waitresses end up putting three tables together for our group. I sit between Andria and Raine, who are both begging me to tell them what happened in the parking lot today with Caleb.

"He's in a band?" Starla exclaims. "How wicked is that!"

Hank takes his baseball cap off and smoothes his hair. It's bright orange now, and shaved in a mohawk. "Yep, I'm in the band too."

Trista punches him in the arm again.

"Do you think he went back home?" I ask Hank. He knows I'm talking about Caleb.

"Yeah. He texted me. He said it didn't go like he thought it would."

"He started texting me when he first got out of jail. I told him then I didn't want to have anything to do with him."

"Our sweet little Natalie, dating a rock star thug?" Starla says. "I would have never guessed!"

Andria glares at Starla, but I don't think anyone else notices. I shrug. "I am an onion," I say. "I have layers."

Two waitresses begin taking our orders, each one at opposite ends of the table. Bethany and Ferris are sitting at the far end, with Peter sitting on the other side of Raine.

Raine makes sure I get the chocolate chip stack. I nudge her. She nudges back. "So Caleb is Natalie's Evil Ex," she prods.

"And there's really nothing more to the story than that," I say. "He went to jail for selling drugs and I broke up with him."

Everyone at the Athens end of the table grows quiet. None of them will add to the story if I don't want them to. They won't mention Winter Oaks or the fact that I had a psychotic break after Caleb gave me ecstasy and I had to go away for my own safety.

Alex sighs. "Actually it was just possession, but still. Caleb has some growing up to do."

I think he feels guilty, that there might have been something he could have done or said to stop Caleb from partying. But Caleb wasn't ready to stop yet. I still don't think he's hit bottom.

I glance over at David, who winks at me in a very Colton-ish manner. I smile at both of them.

It gets late and Ferris and Bethany pay their bills and leave. Peter gives Raine such a spectacular goodbye kiss, she decides to leave with him. She hugs me and Starla. "See y'all tomorrow." She waves at Tris and Andria on her way out, holding Peter's hand.

"So, after IHOP, are we all going to go get drunk?" Starla asks. "I know a great place where we can hang out."

Colton grins. "I still have the keys to the theater."

"And I still have the booze," Starla says.

"Booze sounds awesome," Hank says as he puts his arm around Trista. "We have a hotel room for the night."

"That my sister booked for us," Trista says. "We're not bringing a party there."

"Hanging out in an empty theater sounds like fun," Andria says. "I've heard lots of old Savannah buildings are haunted. Any ghosts?"

Oh hell.

Starla grins. And Colton puts his arm around David, who is shaking his head to keep from laughing. "You'll just have to see for yourself, won't you?"

Sometimes Starla and Colton remind me of Team Rocket. Fabulously evil. And I worry for all the poor little Pokémon that get in their way.

CHAPTER 21

It's almost midnight by the time we make it back to the theater. Exhausted from the play and all the earlier drama with Caleb and Lucas, now I'm full of pancakes and I'd give anything to just go home and crawl into bed.

But Andria and Tris are leaving first thing in the morning, and I want to hang out with them as long as possible.

Colton unlocks the backstage door. Starla digs two bottles out from under her front seat. Vodka and Crown. "Drink machine is down the hall to your left," Colton says.

"I wish I still had that ghost hunting equipment," Starla says, pouting.

It would totally make my night if we all saw some sort of paranormal activity. It would be nice to think maybe I'm not so crazy after all. But I remember everything I read online. There are no ghosts in this theater. It was all in my head. Although I love Starla for still believing the ghost is here.

Starla hands me a Diet Dr. Pepper with vodka. "I remembered!" she says, grinning.

She did. I would feel bad if I turned it down. And it's been hours since I took my medicine. Surely it won't hurt. I take a sip and clink my plastic bottle to hers. "Cheers."

"This is so cool!" Andria says, looking around the stage. "I've never been in an empty theater before." She and Alex grab sodas, but neither of them take the booze Starla is offering. Tris and Hank do.

"Since we're not driving," Hank says.

I watch Colton and David pour out half of their sodas in the water fountain and fill their bottles back up with vodka. I frown. Someone is going to have to drive everyone home.

Not Starla, who's trying to finish her bottle of Crown all by herself. And definitely not me. Andria has enough on her hands with Hank and Tris. I pull out my phone.

Obviously alcohol blesses me with stellar judgment. I sit on the side of the stage and call Lucas.

He answers on the first ring. "What's wrong?"

I should tell him why I'll never forgive Caleb even if I don't have feelings for him anymore. Tell Lucas that I never should have let him say goodbye to me earlier today (or yesterday, since it's now after midnight), and that maybe I might be falling in love with him.

But instead, I just ask, "Can you come back to the theater? David and Colton are too drunk to drive anyone home."

"Hell," he says, with a long sigh. "All right."

And he hangs up on me.

I deserve that. I take another sip of my Dr. Pepper, looking for the courage to say what I need to say when he gets here.

Starla and Colton are telling everyone about the night we used the Ouija board. Yes, I say, it is a shame that we don't have the board with us right now. But of course I don't mean that. A séance might just lead to more hallucinations.

I keep watching the door, waiting for Lucas to show up. I check it twice, to make sure it's unlocked, but I don't want to be waiting in the hallway for him by myself.

Of course, the third time I go to check the door, he's just walking in.

"Oh good, you're here," I say, twisting the cap on my bottle. "I'll just go get the others."

"Nat, wait. We need to talk."

"I'm sorry. I didn't know anyone else to call. Raine went home with Peter and I didn't want to bother them. Andria and Alex aren't drinking, but they're going to have their hands full with Trista and Hank."

"Just how many people are here?" Lucas asks, walking closer to me. We're standing inches apart now. Close enough to touch, if we wanted.

"Star, David, Colton, me," I start listing on my fingers, "Andria, Alex, Hank, and Tris."

"Your friend Caleb didn't stay?" His face is wary. Hopeful.

"I haven't seen him since this afternoon. I wish I'd told you about him sooner. But I really have my reasons for trying to forget he even exists."

Lucas stares at me. "Did he hurt you?"

I stare back, blinking much slower than I normally would. His eyes are so gorgeous.

Lucas takes the soda bottle out of my hand, rescuing it from my nervous twisting, and sets it down on the ground. Then he takes both of my hands in his. "Nat, is that why you had to go to Winter Oaks? Did he hurt you?"

I nod, and Lucas pulls me into his arms. But I push him back, shaking my head as I finally realize what he means. "No, he didn't . . . I mean, we—" I stop myself from telling him yes, Caleb and I had sex, lots of times, but I don't think he needs to hear that right now. As I look up at him, I'm suddenly wondering about him and Starla, and know they've slept together too. And now I don't want to go back out there in the auditorium where I'll have to look at her and imagine them touching each other in Lucas's bed. The thought makes me want to cry.

Lucas pulls me back to his chest, his hands tangling up in my curls. "I'm sorry, Nat. Whatever he did, it's none of my business. I shouldn't have asked."

"No, I think you should know," I say into his shirt sleeve, my fingers curling around the fabric. "You told me your story. You deserve to hear mine." I take a deep breath. "We were at a bonfire during spring break and Caleb gave me ecstasy. I started hallucinating and I thought I saw something climbing up the side of my house. Or someone."

I scared the hell out of my parents that night. They rushed into my bedroom to find me screaming at the top of my lungs about the Spider Person outside my window. Not Spider-Man, because that would have just been silly. But a giant spider that kept calling my name, asking me to open the window.

Lucas rubs my back and I'm so scared he's going to run away if I keep talking, but I have to get it all out. "That's why I ended up at Winter Oaks. So I guess if it weren't for Caleb and his X, I wouldn't have met you."

"And your grandmother has schizophrenia."

I nod. "When my grandfather died, we moved here to help take care of her. She refused to take her meds anymore. I inherited the genes from her, so I probably would have gone psycho one day even without the X, but now I'll never know."

"You're not psychotic, Nat." He pulls away from me so I can see his face. His beautiful hazel eyes. "Just a little crazy. But I'm a little crazy too, so don't you think we belong together?"

My heart actually does a little dance. I try to make it stop. "You have more than enough on your plate right now. You deserve a sane, grounded person who doesn't add drama to your life. You need a low-maintenance girlfriend."

"Like someone who's willing to crawl out of bed with a

raging hangover and babysit when I'm having a crisis?" He smiles down at me. I smile back, even though I have the tiniest of tears beading up in the corners of my eyes. He spots them and wipes them away with his fingers. His fingers are now covered with glitter.

"Oh my God, what kind of low maintenance girlfriend makes you leave your sister at home alone in the middle of the night, just so you can rescue her and her drunk friends?" I'm already terrible at this. "You need to get back home to her."

He rolls his eyes. "Come home with me. We can leave the rest of these drunks here to fend for themselves."

Surely he doesn't mean what I think he means when he says come home with me, but my heart still speeds up.

"Nat!" David shouts, poking his head into the hallway. "We've been looking all over for you! Who's out here with you? Did you find your ghost?" He squints his eyes.

"Yes," Lucas says in a deep voice. "I'm taking Natalie and there's nothing you can do about it."

I hide my face in his shirt to keep from giggling.

"Shit! Colton!" David shouts.

"Oh God," I whisper. "They're all coming out here now. You're doomed."

I feel Lucas's laughter in his chest. "Can we take them home now? Then we'll go back to my house."

"Lucas!" Starla squeals when she sees him. "That's not a ghost, David."

Andria pops her head around the corner too, pulling Alex along with her. She raises her eyebrow at me and I give her the slightest nod. Yes, this is my Mr. Someone Else. At least I'd certainly like for him to be.

I introduce Lucas to my friends from Athens, and Alex rounds up his gang to take them back to their hotel room. Lucas convinces Colton and David we need to take them back to their dorm.

Starla pouts. "But we still haven't seen a real ghost. Natalie is certain there's one here."

I frown at her. "I don't think there is after all. We need to get some sleep before tonight's show."

Colton drags her outside and locks up behind us. "Let us know if Calcifer ever decides to play here in Savannah. We'll make another night of it."

"Or, we could take a road trip to Athens and party up there," Starla says, putting her arms around Lucas when she sees me move away to hug Trista.

Alex puts his arm around Andria, as if he's afraid Starla is going to start grabbing random people. "That sounds great."

Andria manages to hug me despite Alex's grip on her. "Hope we see you again soon!"

Even Hank hugs me. "Take care, Nat." He shakes Lucas's hand. "Nice to meet you, even though I probably won't remember you in the morning."

Lucas shrugs. He laces his fingers into mine. No one notices. "Everyone ready?"

We have three drunk people to transport. And Lucas shoves them all into the backseat.

David and Colton get dropped off first at the SCAD dorm.

Lucas heads back toward his neighborhood. Hope surges in my chest.

"Shouldn't you be dropping off Natalie next?" Starla says. She's lying horizontally across the backseat, now that she has it all to herself. "She lives way over by Forsythe Park."

"But she's not going home," Lucas says, looking at me.

I can't stop the stupidest grin from stretching across my face. I know it's not the most seductive look, but I can't help it. He wants me to go home with him. Starla falls off the seat, but doesn't say anything else. I'm scared she's going to throw up back there, and Lucas will have to clean it up.

He pulls up in front in his own driveway. "Wake up, Star. We're home."

She sits up and blinks. I think she's been crying.

"Are you okay?" I ask.

"I'm fine." She gets out of the car and slams the door shut.

I watch her stumble across the yard to her house, and we wait in the truck until she gets inside safely.

Lucas picks up my hand. "Do you mind sleeping over? I'm really tired, and I don't know if I could drive all the way across town again tonight." He's grinning. If I wanted to go home, he would definitely be a gentleman and take me.

"Are you sure your dad won't mind?"

He shrugs. "He won't notice."

I choose not to think about how many times Starla has spent the night over here. Instead I choose to worry about what I'll say to Mom and Dad in the morning. That I stayed with David at his dorm? He might cover for me. But then again, he might decide to kill Lucas instead.

I pull my phone out and send him a text. *If Mom asks, I'm spending the night w/ U.*

David's still awake. *K.*

A minute later he sends one more text. *Tell him 2 use a condom.*

Oh for the love of naked mole rats. I send Mom a quick text telling her I'm at David's dorm for the night and turn my phone off, blushing. I'm going to get an earful the next time I see my brother. The alcohol buzz I was feeling earlier has long since evaporated. I follow Lucas into his house and down the hallway to his bedroom.

He kisses me on the lips, briefly, and says, "Stay here." He goes to the bedroom next door to check on Caitlyn.

I sit down on his bed, which is indeed bigger than his sister's, thank goodness. The sheets and plaid comforter smell clean. His room is neat. Much neater than I would have expected. A basket of clean clothes sits on the floor at the foot of the bed. I grab the towels on top and begin to fold them out of nervousness.

He comes back in his room to find I've folded half the stuff in the basket. "Seriously? That's not why I brought you to my lair."

"I know," I sigh, smoothing his already wrinkle-free comforter with my hand. "It was so I could make you breakfast, right?"

He takes the clothes and puts them back in the basket carefully before sitting down next to me. "Of course." He leans his head closer. His lips are inches away from mine. "I like my eggs scrambled."

"Noted."

Lucas pushes me back against his pillows gently. He lies between my legs, I lie between his arms, and we can't stop kissing.

"Are we going too fast?" he asks, his fingers gently sliding under my shirt, under my bra straps. My skin is scorched from his touch.

"Lucas Grant, I've wanted to kiss you since the day you delivered pizza to my house."

"Just kissing?" He smiles and my world rocks. His hands slide down my arms, over my hips. "And how long have you wanted to do this with me?"

I touch his face, push his beautiful blond hair out of his eyes. "Since I saw you in that skimpy little Hercules costume."

His eyes light up. "I couldn't keep my eyes off of you in that dress. Do you know how hard it was to remember my lines during the dress rehearsal?"

"And you went to so much trouble to help me remember mine!"

"That wasn't any trouble." He smiles and only stops kissing

me when he reaches over on his nightstand for a tiny square package. "Any excuse I can find to touch you, to be close to you, I'll take it."

Everything this boy says—everything he does—takes my breath away. "You don't need any excuses," I tell him. "I'm right here."

"Yes, you are." His fingers trace shapes on my skin. I shiver, even though I'm not cold.

I pull his head down to mine. And we show each other everything we've been wanting to do to each other.

CHAPTER 22

Caitlyn finds us in the morning, wrapped up under Lucas's comforter. "Natalie! You spent the night! You could have slept with me!"

She jumps on the bed while Lucas rolls over and groans. "Want some breakfast?" she asks me.

"Nat's going to make us scrambled eggs," he mutters from under his pillow. I pinch his butt and he yelps.

"Would you like scrambled eggs?" I ask Caitlyn.

"No, I want the fairy cereal!" She takes off for the kitchen without us.

I really don't know how to make scrambled eggs. Mom is the gourmet in our house. Next time I'll remember to bring cupcakes with me.

Assuming there is a next time. I glance at Lucas, still hiding from the light of day. Is he having regrets? "Do you have to go to work today?" I ask him.

He lifts his hand to my hair, where there is still glitter. I've left glitter all over his pillows. "No, we don't have to be anywhere until the show tonight."

I press a kiss on his shoulder. I need to get home. And face whatever consequences are waiting for me. I throw my clothes back on before Caitlyn can come back.

Lucas and Caitlyn both drive me home after we all share a quick breakfast of cold pizza and cereal. He pulls his truck up in front of my house, behind the line of family cars parked out in the street. I take a deep breath. Maybe everyone is still asleep.

"Can you come back tonight?" Caitlyn asks from the seat between us.

I blush, but can't help looking over at Lucas. He's blushing too, and it makes my head feel floaty. "We'll see," I say, opening the car door.

Lucas reaches around behind his sister to give my curls a tug. "Need a ride to the theater tonight?"

"Raine said she could come and get me if David wasn't willing."

"Don't be silly," Lucas says. "We would be honored to pick up the Fairy Queen."

"Then I'll see you around six?" I ask, opening my door.

Lucas smiles at me, his hazel eyes blazing. "It's a date."

I feel like I'm floating as I walk up the steps to our front door and put my key in the lock. I turn to wave at Caitlyn and Lucas one last time and suddenly I can hear my parents yelling before I've even got the door open.

Crap. They are definitely awake. The floaty feeling evaporates and now my chest is heavy with dread as I go inside. The smell of burnt something hits me. Carrot cake? Spice cake? Oh no.

Mom is in the kitchen banging things around. Dad is standing in the hallway in his wrinkled green scrubs, rubbing his head. "I don't know what else you want me to say."

"I don't want you to say anything." Mom's voice is quiet but deadly. Defeated.

"Elaine," Dad says, sighing. He looks up and sees me. And sighs again. "Hey kiddo. Sorry about last night. How did it go?"

"It's okay, I understand," I say.

"She was magnificent," Grandma says, coming down the stairs. She looks at me. "Did your brother get a new car? That wasn't his old truck you got out of this morning."

My stomach twists. I am so busted. I stare from her to Dad, trying to come up with an explanation before Mom comes out here, too, and they both start yelling at me.

But Mom is too angry to pay attention to Grandma. She yells from the kitchen, "Troy, did you just hear your daughter? She shouldn't have to be understanding and forgiving when you miss important events in her life."

Dad ignores me and Grandma and steps into the kitchen to answer Mom. "If you want me to feel like the world's worst father, then congratulations. I already do. And the world's worst husband. And the world's worst son."

My heart breaks for my dad. And for my mom. I hate that they are both so unhappy right now. I glare at Grandma and try to move past her toward the stairs.

Grandma smirks. "If David would just fix that damn car out there for you, you wouldn't have to be getting rides from strange boys."

I spin around. "Grandma, please." My parents are still yelling in the kitchen and I'm exhausted from last night and now I'm terrified that she is going to say something that will get me grounded until I'm thirty. And probably make my parents yell even more. "He's a good friend," I whisper. "Please don't say anything."

She rolls her eyes. "Just promise me you'll be careful?"

"I promise." When she nods, I give her a quick thanks and run upstairs to my room. I flop down on my bed without bothering to change into my pajamas. I fall asleep almost immediately, with the muffled sounds of Mom and Dad still arguing downstairs.

I wake up before my alarm goes off, because Mom is sitting on my bed again. "Natalie?"

I sit up, shocked to see her looking calm. And maybe happy? "Are you okay?" I ask.

Her face relaxes into a smile. "I think your father and I just need to take some time for ourselves and get away. Ms. Susan next door has offered to stay here with Grandma tonight. We're driving over to Hilton Head to stay for the night. Just the two of us."

This is much better news than anything I was expecting to hear. "You deserve a break, Mom. And so does Dad. You need to have some fun."

"David is going to be coming home with you after the play so he can keep an eye on Grandma, and so Ms. Susan can go home. Will you please not drive your brother crazy?"

"Do you promise he won't drive me crazy?"

Mom leans over and kisses me on the cheek. "I love you."

"Have a good trip," I tell her, hugging her. I can't wait to tell David the good news.

CHAPTER 23

And run through fire I will, for thy sweet sake,
—*A Midsummer Night's Dream*, act 2, scene 2

I am useless tonight. All I can think of is Lucas. His scent, his touch, his kisses. How soon I can be back in his arms again. I'm going to ruin the show with a distracted, moony-eyed Titania. I've already stepped on my own costume twice, tearing the hem and causing Melinda to have kittens. The flowers for my hair are missing and now goth girl is threatening dreadlocks again. The fact that we really don't have time for her to backcomb all of my hair is the only reason I manage to stay dread-free.

Starla offers to help put my hair up in a twist, but goth girl shoos her out of the dressing room. Starla comes back not ten minutes later with a tiara to replace the missing flowers.

"Every queen should have a crown," she says, running her fingers through my hair.

It looks beautiful.

"So, are you ready to talk about what happened with you and Lucas last night?" She is smiling at me in the mirror, but it looks forced. She's trying hard to accept that Lucas is moving on. And I hate that I've broken one of the sacred girl rules by falling in love with her ex.

"I'm so sorry," I say.

She squeezes my bare shoulders. Hard. "Don't be sorry. He deserves a nice girl like you. I've moved on too, you know. It was for the best."

While I wonder if it's Hunter she's moved on with, I can't help but ask, "Why did you and Lucas break up?"

"It's complicated," she says sadly. "I never felt like my love was enough for him."

Raine snorts. "Because you didn't only love him, Starla. You also loved Michael and Fer—"

Starla elbows Raine in the stomach as Mrs. Green sweeps into the dressing room.

From the corner of my eye, I see something dark scurry across the mirror. When I turn my head, it's gone. It must have been my imagination. Mrs. Green is telling us how important tonight is for the fund-raiser.

I nod, worried about the dark thing in the mirror. There are no ghosts here.

I stare at the mirror and the dark shadow behind Mrs. Green's reflection grows. I gasp.

"Darling, are you all right?" she asks.

I shudder. "Yes, ma'am." Did I take my medicine yesterday? Or the day before? Oh no. I can't remember.

Her cell phone chimes. She gives my shoulder a gentle squeeze before answering. There is a minor crisis in the sound booth and she is needed up there immediately.

Raine crosses her arms. "You look nervous. Want something to drink? Just a little bit?"

I shake my head. Trying to avoid making a fool out of myself will be hard enough sober. "I'll be fine once I get back into character." Titania doesn't have the same problems that

Natalie has. Just a psychotic fairy husband who drugs her to get his way.

"I know a way to help you with that," Starla says. She opens the closet and rummages through the hanging garments until she finds a long silk scarf. It's a green paisley and I don't think it goes with my costume at all.

"There was a famous actress in Russia who used this technique to help her focus." She places the scarf over my head. "It helps to block everything else out of your mind. Close your eyes."

Even though the scarf is light, it does make me feel cut off from everything.

"Sort of like a sensory deprivation chamber," Raine says. "Huh." She stares at Starla with her arms crossed.

"Exactly," Starla says. "Take a deep breath, Natalie, and focus on Titania. We'll leave you alone so you can concentrate."

I don't know if I want to be alone right now, but I thank them anyway. I close my eyes. I can't take a deep breath because the scarf smells like moth balls and gives me a headache. I am not thinking about Titania. I am thinking about being able to breathe.

I pull the scarf off my head, but Starla has turned the light off too, and with no window in the room, it's pitch black. I stumble toward the wall, feeling for the light switch.

I find the doorknob before I find the light, but it won't turn.

This is stupid. The dressing room should lock from inside, but I can't get it to open. The lock on the door knob spins uselessly when I turn it.

There's a noise above me, coming from the air conditioner vent. The ancient air conditioner turns on, I believe, but the noise begins to sound like a low voice. Moaning.

"Stop it!" I scream.

The doorknob behind me begins to shake. Someone is out in the hall.

I beat against the door with the palm of my hand. "It's stuck! I can't get out!"

The doorknob stops. It grows silent in the hallway.

I try opening the door again, but it's still locked.

I'm worried about the time, but I have no idea where my phone is. My purse was on the dressing table, so I stumble across the room, hoping I'm headed in the right direction.

I hold my skirt up so I don't trip, but bang my knee against a chair.

"Dammit!" I scream. I feel for my purse and accidentally knock it off the counter in my clumsiness. I drop down to the floor, my hands outstretched until I feel the familiar leather strap. Or is it a strap? I drop it, certain it just hissed at me.

The room is silent again, except for my hard breathing. What is wrong with me? Even in the darkness, I know there's nothing dangerous in this dressing room. But knowing and believing are two different things.

I reach out for my purse again, tentatively. Yes, I'm certain it's my purse, and I rummage through it searching for my phone.

I have no idea what time it is, or how long until the curtain goes up. I'm sure I need to hurry. That someone is going to notice me missing any time now.

I can't find my phone. I am trying not to panic.

Why would Starla do this? Did she lock me in here on purpose? What did she tell her aunt?

Will Lucas come looking for me?

I turn my purse over, shaking it until everything is out on the floor in front of me. I run my hand back and forth, searching. My phone has got to be here.

But it's not. I've become more angry now than scared. I stand up again and try to find the light switch. I misjudge the distance and stub my toe on the wall. I'm going to look like I've been beaten up by the time I make it on to the stage.

I find the light switch, finally. The dressing room is flooded in fluorescent light and I blink. Then I scream. On the mirror, in dripping red letters, are the words "Crazy Bitch."

I slide down the closed door, trying to take deep breaths. *I'm not crazy. I'm not crazy.*

I can't help the sob that comes out of my chest.

"Natalie?" It's Lucas calling from the hallway. "Mrs. Green is looking for you!"

I turn around and beat on the door. "I'm stuck! The door won't open!"

Crazy Bitch.

No. I'm not crazy!

"Nat?" Lucas's voice is closer now. "What do you mean you're stuck? The lock is on the inside."

"I think it's broken. It won't unlock."

He jiggles the doorknob, to test for himself. "All right, I'll be back with someone to help. Are you okay?"

I stare at the words on the mirror once more. Crazy Bitch.

"Yes," I lie.

I'm mad at myself for screaming, but I'm shaking all over. That can't be blood. It has to be paint. Or . . . I make myself go closer to investigate . . . food coloring?

What the hell?

Giggling behind me makes me shriek again. The noise is coming from the closet.

I'm shaking I'm so angry and so frightened. What is happening? This is no ghost. I don't think it's a hallucination, either.

My heart is pounding so hard I think I'm going to throw up.

I hear the giggling again and I take a step toward the closet. Am I hearing things? It doesn't sound very ghostly. In fact, I think I recognize that voice.

I tear the closet door open.

Starla falls out, laughing so hard she is clutching her stomach. "Oh my God! You should see your face! This is too funny!"

"Starla?" I stare at her, feeling cold and hot at the same time. "What are you doing?"

She picks herself up, straightening out her gown. "I don't know what you're talking about."

"You locked me in here."

"Why would I do that?"

A light in the back of the closet draws my attention. It's coming from an open door at the opposite end, leading into the bathroom. How did I not notice before the rooms were connected by the extra-large wardrobe closet?

"You wrote that on the mirror," I say, pointing to the red mess that isn't legible anymore. "And the handprints the other day in the bathroom."

Starla looks at me with pity in her eyes. "Nat. It's okay. You can trust me."

I realized she'd been hiding in the closet that day, too. "How did you make the fake blood?"

She smiles smugly. "It pays to have friends in the makeup department at SCAD. They know just how to whip up a batch of fake blood and which makeup remover wipes are scent free and leave no streaks on a mirror."

"Let me out of here," I say, backing toward the door. "Show me how to fix the door."

"I really don't know what you're rambling about, Natalie."

"Why are you trying to make me think I'm losing my mind?"

"There you go, rambling again." Starla takes a step toward me. "You're starting to worry me."

"Natalie?" Lucas's voice makes me relax a little. "Still doing okay?"

"I'm fi—"

"Lucas! Natalie's going to hurt me!" Starla screams. "She locked me in here with her!"

I stare at my friend in shock. My blood runs cold. She's not my friend anymore. And she probably never was. "I don't feel safe in here," Starla says, her eyes glittering with hatred.

"Why would you say that?" I ask. "You've been doing this all along. There was no ghost. It was you. I thought I was seeing things. Hearing things. And it was you all along."

My throat feels heavy. My eyes sting, but I'll be damned if she'll see me cry. "Why would you do this?"

She grabs my hands and swings me away from the door. I'm too startled to scream. "Lucas was mine until you moved to town," she hisses.

"But you broke up with him. You didn't want him anymore."

"That doesn't matter." Her fingernails tear at the skin on my wrists. She raises her voice. "Lucas, she's trying to hurt herself. I'm afraid she's going to hurt me next."

"Natalie? What's going on in there?" Lucas is beating on the door.

How can I defend myself against Starla?

"I know all about your craziness, psycho. It's been so funny watching you try to hide it all summer."

"You knew?" My head is reeling. I don't know why she's attacking me and have no clue how to defend myself.

"Natalie?" Mrs. Green is now outside the dressing room with Lucas. "Please open this door right now."

"It's stuck!" I shout. "Starla did something to the lock."

"She's lying, Aunt Carol!" Starla is glaring at me. "I saw you last spring when I went to visit Lucas at that horrible place," she hisses. "I recognized you when you first showed up at the Pirate House."

"O . . . kay, why are you telling me this now? Why would you keep it a secret for so long? And why, for the love of Shakespeare and all that is holy, would you wait until right now to attack me?"

There is an awful noise on the other side of the door. I don't know if they're trying to kick it down or dismantle it. The screws for the doorknob are on this side. The hinges are on this side.

Starla shrugs. "Why do crazy people do the things they do, Natalie? I can't even begin to guess how your weird little mind works."

"Starla, open the door before they break it down."

"I didn't do anything. What did you do to that door, Natalie?"

The door shudders. I hear Mrs. Green and Lucas yelling, but I can't understand what they're saying anymore. I don't understand any of this. Starla has been messing with my head all this time. She wanted me to think I was psychotic. My legs give out from under me and I find myself sitting on the floor.

The door bursts open and Starla throws herself down on the floor, too. "She hit me!" she wails. "Oh God, Natalie! I thought we were friends!"

Mrs. Green and Lucas both run to check on Starla. Wonderful. In the hallway, I see several cast members peeking in the door at the drama. Caitlyn stands next to Raine, both of them staring at me in shock.

"I didn't do anything to her!" I say. "She's lying."

Mrs. Green comes over and stands above me. "Young lady, what is going on here?"

I always thought our theater director was an intelligent, fair-minded person. But as I look around the room, seeing Starla sobbing in Lucas's arms, I get angry.

"She covered my head with a scarf and turned out the lights and hid in the closet to scare me. She broke the lock on the door somehow, so I couldn't leave, and when I turned the light on, the writing on the mirror was there."

Everyone turns to look at the mirror. It's just a runny, red mess now, but you can still see what the words were.

Crazy Bitch.

Everyone is staring at me now.

Oh God, I sound just like a crazy person.

Starla sobs, holding on to Lucas.

Mrs. Green reaches her hand out toward me, to help me up. "Miss Roman, I think we need to call your parents. I don't think you're in any shape to perform tonight."

I really can't argue with that, but I don't want her to bother Mom or Dad right now. Not when they are finally getting a chance to be alone together.

"But what about the play?" Starla cries. "Who will play Titania?"

Mrs. Green folds her arms. "Run and get Maizy from the sound booth. She's the Cast Three Titania. If she can't do it, we'll just have to cancel tonight's performance."

"No!" Caitlyn yells in the hallway. Her fairy wings shake as she stomps her feet in anger. "This is all your fault!" she says, glaring at me before taking off.

"Dammit," Lucas says, leaving Starla to go after his sister.

There is no way I'll ever be able to prove this is not my fault. Everyone is going to be mad at me for ruining the play. I put my head on my knees.

"Miss Roman, would you be so kind as to give Melinda your gown and change back into your own clothes while I call your parents?"

"Of course," I whisper. But now there is no door and I have no privacy.

Raine helps Starla stand and the two of them leave, with only a few suspicious glares in my direction.

Melinda pushes her way through the crowd into the dressing room. She pulls out a folding screen and sets it up so I can change behind it.

I try not to get any tears or snot on THE DRESS. It's breaking my heart that I'll never get to wear it again. Or possibly it's breaking because I'll never see Lucas again. Or because all my friends are scared of me. Or because some of them actually hate me.

Once I change into jeans and a T-shirt, I slip my sandals on and search for Raine. I want to know if she's been in on Starla's tricks this whole, time too.

Raine and Peter are standing in the hallway backstage. "Where's Starla?" I ask her.

She stands up, defensive, and Peter joins her. "In the office with Colton and Mrs. Green. What did you do to her?" God, she looks like she thinks I'm going to attack her.

She breaks my heart, too. "Why are you so quick to believe that I did something to her?" I ask. "Were you in on it, too?"

"What are you talking about?" Peter asks.

"She's been tricking me this whole time, trying to make me think I'm going crazy."

Raine bites her lip. She looks uncertain, hesitant. "Natalie, listen to yourself. Why would Starla want you to think you're crazy?"

I don't know whom to trust anymore.

"Where is David?" I ask. At least my brother will believe me. I think.

Peter nods toward the front of the theater. "He took over the sound booth since Maizy has to play Titania tonight."

Mrs. Green comes out of her office and glares at me. "Your grandmother is coming to pick you up."

Raine and Peter are forgotten. "No, she can't drive!" I say. "Where are my parents?"

She crosses her arms. "Your grandmother answered the house number when I called. She said she'd be here as soon as possible. I'd like for you to go and sit down in the foyer until she comes."

I storm out to the foyer, flop down on a bench, and pull out my phone to call Mom. I don't want them to have to cancel their mini-vacation, but I don't want to be blamed for Grandma driving around loose in Savannah, either.

I could find David, but I don't want to pull him out of the sound booth. That would only make Mrs. Green even angrier.

"Hey." Lucas sits down on the bench next to me. "Are you doing okay?"

"I'm fine." The fact that he's walking on eggshells around me makes me mad. He doesn't trust me either. He thinks I'm unstable.

"Natalie, things have been extremely crazy these past two days. So it's totally understandable if you—"

"It. Wasn't. Me." I look up at him, willing him to believe me. But all I see in his eyes is pity. A layer of frost settles inside my chest. Why should I work so hard to convince Lucas? Why doesn't he believe in me?

He takes a deep breath. "Starla said both of you got locked in the dressing room and you panicked. That it made you have some sort of episode."

"I might have panicked a little when she threw the scarf over my head and turned the lights off, but I did NOT have an episode."

"Why would she do that?" he asks.

"Why don't you ask her?" I snap.

He looks skeptical. Of course he believes her story over mine. Just like everyone else. Why should I even bother defending myself?

"Just forget it." I stand up to go find David and tell him what is going on. Maybe I can talk to him before anyone else does. Maybe he will listen to my side.

"Natalie, wait. Please," he adds, when I don't turn around. "Help me understand." Lucas puts his hand on the door frame above me. "Don't run away."

Anger boils over in my chest. I push him away. I want to tell him that I don't have schizophrenia and that Starla has been trying all along to convince me otherwise. But it sounds like a classic paranoid line a true schizophrenic would say. And I want Lucas to trust me whether I'm sick or not.

The music for the opening starts. I can't bother David now. The play is already beginning and he will be busy.

"Never mind. It's better if you just leave me alone. Tell Caitlyn I'm sorry."

Lucas picks up my hand. I blink back tears and pull my hand away.

He starts to say something, but instead he finally moves away. "I'm sorry, too, Nat."

I wait for him to leave before I let the tears fall. He deserves better, I tell myself. He has enough going on in his life, without a possibly psychotic girlfriend. And a psychotically jealous ex-girlfriend.

I shiver, remembering the cold malice in Starla's eyes. I've seen bullies before, but I've never been attacked so viciously. No one has ever purposely tried to make me doubt my sanity.

I'm still not sure what is real anymore. Ghosts are definitely not real. Love is apparently not real, either. I wipe my cheek on my shirt.

I get up and walk outside. David has probably already heard the story from Colton anyway. And he'll probably call Mom and Dad as soon as he gets a chance.

I don't think Mrs. Green really cares if I sit outside or in the foyer. She just wants me away from the rest of the cast. She might even be worried I'll cause a scene and scare the audience.

The night is muggy, but there's a breeze that carries just a hint of sea air.

I wait. And wait. And worry. Maybe Grandma didn't understand Mrs. Green. Maybe she remembered she didn't have transportation and just went to bed, forgetting about me. If she doesn't come soon, the play will be over and I can go home with David.

I try calling our house phone, but there's no answer. Grandma must have already left. At least I hope she's already left.

Forty minutes later, after I've read three comic books on my phone, my grandmother's silver Jetta, resurrected from the dead, pulls up in front of the theater's entrance. I reach for the handle of the passenger door, and am surprised to see Grandma sitting there. She points to the backseat.

I open the back door instead and climb in, to find Caleb in the driver's seat.

He grins and gives me a jazzy finger wave.

CHAPTER 24

"What the hell are you doing here?" I ask, glaring at Caleb.

"We're rescuing you, Princess," Grandma says. "Tell the nice young man thank you."

Caleb knows better than to expect me to thank him. He pulls back onto the street. "Where to, Mrs. Roman?"

"How did you get this bucket of bolts to run?" I ask. I shouldn't call the car names. Grandma might get insulted and decide not to give it to me after all.

"Did you know your ex-boyfriend was a mechanic?" Grandma is smiling at Caleb, and I feel I have climbed into the weirdest nightmare.

"No. When did you learn to fix cars?"

"In jail. They sent me through a Vo Tech course."

"Made him a productive member of society. How about that." Grandma is deliriously happy to be out of the house. Away from my parents. She's almost giddy.

"Grandma, we need to get back home."

"No, first you need to tell me who that horrid woman was

that called me and what happened. She said you were acting strange."

"No, everyone needs to hold on," Caleb says. "First things first." He pulls into Sonic and orders three chocolate cherry ice cream floats. Without asking us if we even like chocolate cherry ice cream floats. "You need sugar to deal with this." He looks at Grandma. "Do you have any cash on you?"

"Oh, for crying out loud," I say, pulling money out of my wallet.

"Thanks, Nat."

"Is that why you dumped this kid?" Grandma asks. "Because he's a freeloader?"

"I dumped him because he is a drug addict who gave me ecstasy and made me have a psychotic episode."

Caleb has the sense to look sheepish. "I was over at your house when your grandmother got the phone call. I needed to give you this." He hands me an envelope. "Will you read it as soon as you get a chance?"

"And she just happened to ask you to fix her car?" I shove his letter into my purse. I'm in no mood to read anything right now.

"I took the bus here from Athens. I don't have a car. And she didn't have any other way to come and get you. Mrs. Roman was worried about you, Nat."

Our order is here, so he pays the car hop and passes us our floats.

"Now can we go home?" I ask. "Wasn't Ms. Susan staying over at the house with you?" I wonder if our neighbor called my parents. I wonder if my parents have called the house to check on Grandma.

Grandma shakes her head. "Susan fell asleep on the couch not long after Master Chef was over. I told her I was going to bed early, and not to bother me because I had a headache. But

I have some things I need to take care of before we go home. Make a left up here, Caleb."

I'm not about to admit it out loud, but this chocolate Cherry Coke float is delicious.

"Do you know this is the first time I've left the house since your grandfather died?" Grandma says. "I was supposed to do something for him before he was buried and . . ." She sighs, looking out the window. "I should have done this months ago."

"Should have done what?" I ask. She ended up in the hospital for a psych evaluation before Grandpa's funeral. I thought it was terrible that she didn't get the chance to tell him good-bye.

"Never mind. I'm pretty sure we can get this taken care of before anybody misses us. It's a good thing you got kicked out of the theater when you did, Natalie. Excellent timing."

I glare at the back of her head. "Um, happy to help?"

Caleb looks at me in the rearview mirror and grins. Ugh.

"I think we're running out of civilization," Caleb says. We're on Highway 80, and the looming, Spanish moss-covered oak trees have given way to a dark bridge over darker swampy waters.

"Where are we going?" I ask.

"Not far, I promise. Why don't you sit back and read the note this nice young man has written you?"

"It's too dark to read," I grumble. "Mom and Dad are going to kill us."

Grandma doesn't answer. She's too busy humming "Come Together" and while I always thought it was one of the creepier Beatles songs, Grandma actually makes it sound like a demonic chant.

We drive past ritzy waterfront suburbs. No twenty-four-hour convenience stores or even gas stations out here. "Are you sure we have enough gas for this?"

"We'll be fine," Caleb says. As if he knows where he's going.

"I bet this is a pretty drive in the daylight." He starts humming along with Grandma.

Wonderful.

I try not to think about what is going on at the theater. Whether the performance is over yet (which I'm sure it's not) and who is going out to celebrate afterwards.

I look at my phone guiltily. No word from Mom, so she probably hasn't heard from David yet. I should try calling her, but I really don't want to talk to her or Dad just yet. This is all my fault, even if I have been kidnapped by my ex-boyfriend and my schizophrenic grandmother. I don't want to be yelled at until it absolutely can't be helped. I drink the rest of my chocolate cherry float in silence.

It's only a forty-minute drive to Tybee Island, but this is the first time this summer I've been to the beach. We used to come here when I was little and we'd stay during the summer with my grandparents. My heart hurts right now, missing Grandpa so bad. I can't imagine what Grandma is feeling or thinking right now.

I get a text from David demanding to know where I went. I reply that I'm with Grandma, and that we're both fine. I'm sure Colton has told him otherwise.

"Am I turning anytime soon?" Caleb asks. Most of the beach bars are still open, but there is little traffic this time of night.

"Keep going. I'll tell you when to turn." She's stopped humming.

My phone lights up in my lap. A text from Lucas. *Are you okay?*

Fine, I text back.

Can we talk about what happened?

A storm of different emotions slams into me. Hope, fear, confusion, hurt. I'm happy that he's talking to me, but now is not the time. Grandma has finally told Caleb to pull into one of the last parking lots at the very southern end of the island's beach.

"What are we doing here?" I ask, as we all get out of the car. My phone stays on the backseat with my purse.

Grandma wraps her cardigan around her as she heads for the sand dunes. "Keeping a promise. You can come along or wait here. Up to you."

I can't help but glance over at Caleb. He's watching me quietly. I can't even imagine what he's thinking, basically getting kidnapped and taken to the Atlantic Ocean when all he wanted . . .

"It's okay. We'll be right behind you," I tell my grandmother. I cross my arms and glare at my ex. "What do you want, Caleb? Why are you here?"

He laughs, leaning against the hood of the car. "Closure, I guess. Just wanted to make amends. I realized at the theater that you were moving on. At least trying to." He sighs, pushing his hair out of his face. "What I did to you was horrible. I just wanted one more chance to talk to you, to apologize, and to tell you I'd never bother you again."

I take a deep, heavy breath. "I am trying to move on, Caleb. I'm sorry I said I'd never forgive you. I do forgive you. But we're never going to be together." And I know I said that before, but I really mean it this time.

"I kinda figured that." His sad smile breaks my heart and almost changes my mind.

Almost.

Insert long awkward silence here. I look around, searching for Grandma. There's country music spilling out of one of the bars we passed, but there's no one else on the beach at this hour. "We should probably go find her," I say finally.

He follows me across the parking lot and from the steps of

the sea wall we can look down on the beach and see her. She's walking along the water's edge, searching for something.

"Grandma?" I shout into the wind.

"Can we help you find something?" Caleb asks, as I follow him across the dunes.

"What are you looking for?" I ask, stopping just short of where the waves curl up against the sand.

She's walking in the water barefoot, her shoes in her hand. I worry about jellyfish, rusty nails, sharks. "I made him a promise," she says sadly. "And I never got to keep it."

Caleb stares at me. I never told him about my grandmother, although I'm sure he's starting to catch on that she's not normal. I shrug. "What was the promise?"

"When we first got married, we didn't have a lot of money. For our first anniversary, I was in art school and your grandfather had just started working at the hospital. He gave me a wooden box full of sand dollars. Every year after that, we celebrated our anniversary at the beach and gave each other a sand dollar. He asked to be buried with a sand dollar in his hand. And I wasn't there to make sure it happened."

She tucks a silver curl behind her ear and looks out across the waves. "But I can still bring him a sand dollar for our anniversary this year."

Caleb pulls his phone out of his pocket and turns on the flashlight app. A tiny area of the beach lights up.

I wish I hadn't left my phone in the car. The moon is huge tonight and the lights in the parking lot keep it from being too dark, but sand dollars aren't bleached white when you first find them on the beach. I remember this from the summers spent out here with my grandparents. A living sand dollar is purple and fuzzy. The exoskeletons that you can buy in any beach side gift shop have been bleached and treated. They are originally brown and fragile.

Grandma used to call them mermaid coins when David and I were little.

"Is this one?" Caleb asks, splashing his hand in the water.

Grandma and I join him and peer into his hand.

"You picked up a jellyfish!" I squeal.

Caleb drops it and jumps back. "Gross!"

"Does your hand itch?" Grandma says. "Rub some sand on your palm to take out some of the sting."

Caleb is washing his hand back and forth in the surf. "I don't think I felt anything. It was just cold." He shines his light up and down the shoreline.

Grandma keeps us out here for hours searching in the dark water. Surely by now the play is over. David will be home soon looking for me. He'll find both me and Grandma missing and will probably assume it's my fault. I pray he hasn't called Mom and Dad.

Caleb doesn't try to talk to me anymore, but instead lends Grandma his phone. She uses the light to search up and down the beach. I pick up a long stick of driftwood and poke the sand as I follow behind both of them.

"Here we go!" Grandma smiles as she bends down.

She picks up two tiny brown sand dollar exoskeletons. Tiny brown corpses. "These are perfect," she says, gently brushing the sand off of them. "Now let's head back to the city."

Caleb and I follow her back to the car. "Let Natalie drive back," Grandma says. "This is her car now."

"But I'm not on the insurance yet!" I say. I've been lusting after this car all summer. Even if it is a beat-up four-door hatchback.

"Neither was your friend here," Grandma says. "He didn't let that stop him."

"Actually my license is suspended," Caleb says.

"What? Give me the keys!" I demand, holding my hand out. He just grins and tosses them to me.

I'm nervous but also excited as I buckle myself into the driver's seat. I've had a license since we moved to Savannah, and sometimes David lets me drive his truck. Every once in a while.

Ok, rarely. But I made an A in Driver's Ed and I'm very cautious. I find the headlights, the turn signal, the air conditioner controls.

Caleb reaches up into the front between me and Grandma and plays with the radio.

Grandma pops his hand. "Keep it on the oldies station."

"Fine," he groans, sitting back down.

"Home?" I ask, turning the key in the ignition. The car does not start.

"Uh-oh," Caleb says.

"Are you kidding?" I glare at him in the rearview mirror. "I thought you fixed it."

"Pop the hood," he says, sliding out of the backseat.

I open the hood for him and sigh, leaning my forehead against the steering wheel.

"It'll be fine," Grandma says. "It didn't take him too long to fix it last time."

"Can someone come out here and hold a light up so I can see?" Caleb shouts. "This was much easier to do when the sun was shining."

I get out and turn on the flashlight app on my phone. "Thanks," Caleb says. "I guess I didn't have the cables attached tight enough. Sorry about that."

But the battery cables aren't loose. And when he tries to crank the car, he just shakes his head. "It's out of gas. I don't suppose there's a gas can in the trunk, Mrs. Roman?"

Grandma shrugs.

I roll my eyes and hand Caleb the last of the money I have in my purse.

"Didn't think so," Caleb mutters. "Y'all stay here with the doors locked. I'll be back." He hands me back the keys and I take his place once again in the driver's seat.

Grandma and I sit in the dark for several long minutes after he walks off, neither of us saying anything. Finally, she sighs. Heavily. "Sorry about tonight, Natalie."

I laugh. "Not your fault." I don't even know why she's apologizing.

"John Lennon said there are only two forces in the universe that motivate us: fear and love." My grandmother looks over at me. "Choose love, Natalie. Not fear."

She's right, but I don't want her to know that. I cross my arms and tip my head back against the driver's seat. "I'm not choosing Caleb," I say.

My grandmother cracks up. "I know, baby. You deserve so much more. And I know you have the courage to fight for what you deserve. Don't be afraid to live your life. No matter what comes."

And that's the end of my crazy but wise old grandmother's heart-to-heart talk. She starts humming along with the radio again, but is soon snoring softly with her head leaning against the window.

I might drift off too, because I scream when Caleb taps on my window.

Grandma mumbles something I'm sure grandmothers aren't supposed to say.

"Sorry," Caleb says. "Did you know there's only one gas station on this freaking island that's open 24 hours?"

"Let me guess," I say, as I pop the gas door open for him. "It wasn't the one closest to us?"

"Of course not." He unscrews the cap and fills the tank.

The gasoline vapors give me an instant headache. "Do I have any change?" I ask.

My ex-boyfriend just shrugs. "Island gas is expensive." He puts the empty can in the trunk and hops back into the backseat. "And the adventure can continue," he says, patting the back of my seat.

"Finally," I grumble as I pull back onto the highway. The sky is starting to get light. Oh my God, we've been out all night.

"One more stop," Grandma says. "We need to go to Bonaventure."

"Wait, what?" I ask.

"The cemetery?" Caleb asks. "Cool. Hey, Lucas wants to know where you are. Want me to text him back?"

He's frowning as he scrolls through my phone. "Give me that!" I reach behind me with one hand.

"Ten and Two!" Grandma yells. "Keep both hands on the steering wheel!"

I can't reach Caleb as he's scooted over to the far side of the backseat, behind Grandma. I wish I'd just turned my phone off earlier. I don't want to deal with Lucas right now.

"Hey, Lover! We are heading back from the beach with Grandma. Wish U were here!" Caleb says, texting.

"Caleb, don't you dare," I say.

He laughs. "Just kidding. You really don't want to answer him?"

I grip the steering wheel. "No."

"Okay." I hear my phone turn off.

"Thanks."

"Are you lovers?" Grandma asks.

My face burns, and Caleb mumbles, "Don't answer that. I really don't want to know."

And the awkwardness gets even worse until Grandma turns the volume up on the radio. I'm grateful. By the time we've heard a Joni Mitchell song, a Doors triple play, and "American Pie," we're back within the city limits. We all sing along to "American Pie."

"Take a right at this next light," Grandma tells me.

I keep following her instructions and soon we're pulling into the empty parking lot at Bonaventure Cemetery.

Almost empty. There are two other vehicles here. One that belongs to the city, and the other, an old dusty Toyota.

Caleb peeks out the window. "Whoah. Creepy trees."

Grandma just smiles. "Come on, we've got some walking to do."

It really is a hike to get to the newer sections of Savannah's famous cemetery. Grandma wasn't well enough to come to Grandpa's funeral, but most of his family is buried out here, so she knows where his headstone is. Caleb and I follow her in silence.

It's quiet and beautiful, with just a hint of early morning mist that is burning off slowly. The only sound is the crunch of our feet on the gravel path.

Finally, we reach the end of a curving lane and the thick trees give way to a view of the river. I grab Caleb by the arm to pull him back. I think Grandma might need a few minutes by herself. But she's already forgotten about us. She takes the shells she's been holding all this time and places them gently on top of the headstone.

A man and a little girl are standing at a grave not far from Grandpa's. It's Caitlyn and her father.

Caitlyn spots me immediately. "Natalie!" She flies across the grass and attacks me with a hug.

"You find friends in the strangest places," Caleb says.

"Dad wanted to talk to Mom this morning. I told him I

had to come, too." She looks up at Caleb suspiciously. "Who are you?"

"One of Natalie's strange friends," he says, grinning.

She looks at him. "You *are* strange."

"He's in a band," I tell her, as if that explains everything. "Does Lucas know you two are out here?"

"He had to go to work early this morning. To help clean the pool."

I glance over at the man kneeling at the headstone. I don't know if I should text Lucas, or mind my own business.

Caitlyn starts telling Caleb about being a fairy in the play. And the Midsummer Night's Ball. "Lucas said I'm too young to go to the ball, but Hailey and Bailey are going and they didn't even come to the performances."

"Do you have to be a fairy to go to the ball?" Caleb asks.

"Of course not. Mrs. Green says the mayor is supposed to be there."

"It's just a stupid fund-raiser for the city," I tell him. "I'm not going either, Caitlyn."

"Why not?"

"Because I am tired of playing fairy queen. I just want to go home and sleep for the next month."

"Maybe you're just depressed. Cupcakes would cheer you up."

Caleb snorts and starts heading back to the car.

I take Caitlyn by the hand and bring her back to her father. He's younger-looking than I first thought when I met him at their house. But I see where Lucas gets his kind hazel eyes and where Caitlyn gets her sandy curls.

"This is Natalie," Caitlyn says.

Her father's face lights up. "The cupcake girl."

Oh my God. I'm too busy blushing to say anything.

"Thank you," he says, putting his hands in his pockets.

"My mom is the baker," I finally stammer.

"But you made Lucas happy."

"And me!" Caitlyn says, hugging her dad's leg.

He puts a hand on top of her hair. He looks happy, too. Maybe he's going to start being more of a father now.

And maybe Lucas won't have quite so many things to worry about. And maybe he'll have time for a girlfriend. And maybe he'll forgive me for upsetting Caitlyn.

And maybe I won't screw this up again.

CHAPTER 25

I drop Caleb off at the bus station before taking Grandma home. I surprise myself by giving him a hug. "I'm glad you're not doing drugs anymore."

"You've changed so much since this spring," he says.

"Is that good or bad?"

"You're much stronger. You know what you want. And what you don't want."

"Good-bye, Caleb," I say, and watch him walk inside the bus station. But I don't know if I believe him. Do I really know what I want? Or is it just that I know what I don't want?

Grandma falls asleep again in the ten minutes it takes me to get to the house. I give her shoulder a gentle shake and she wakes up with a start. "We're home," I tell her.

I take a deep breath. It's just after nine in the morning. And I'm sure Grandma and I are both in a lot of trouble. I should have texted Mom last night to tell her where we were. Or David.

"Don't worry," Grandma says. "I'll handle your parents."

That doesn't make me feel any better.

Both Mom's and Dad's cars are parked out front. But we only find Dad in the living room, passed out on the couch. He opens his eyes as soon as he hears us come inside. "Where the hell have you been? We were just about to call the police to help look for you!"

Oh my God. I feel so stupid for worrying them.

"The cemetery," Grandma says. "I made Natalie take me out there to see Jim."

Briefly, the anger in Dad's eyes is replaced with guilt. "Why didn't you call, Mom? I would have taken you."

And I realize my own phone is probably still in the backseat of Grandma's car. "I'll be right back. I need my phone," I say.

Grandma has her hands on her hips, glaring at Dad. I don't want to be here for this anyway. I slip back out the front door and hop down the porch steps.

Lucas is walking up the sidewalk wearing swim shorts and his pool shirt. My heart stops when he sees me. "Hey."

"Hey." I don't know what else to say. Should I still be mad at him? Hurt? Hopeful? I stop walking and cross my arms.

He shoves his hands in his pockets. "I got your message. Are you okay?"

"What message?" I suddenly have a terrible feeling. I stomp over to Grandma's car and open the back door, looking for my phone.

When the screen lights up I see a million *Where are you???* texts from David and a text that was sent to Lucas. *I'm sorry. Can we talk at my house?*

Caleb. The only person I know who texts in all caps. I will kill him if I ever see him again.

I look up at Lucas. He's staring at me uncertainly, and I want nothing more than to wrap my arms around him. To kiss him senseless. "So, I saw your dad this morning. At the cemetery."

His eyebrow rises, and he looks confused. "I haven't seen him leave the house since the funeral. Are you sure it was him?"

I nod. "Caitlyn was with him."

He takes a deep breath. And I reach out and grab his wrist. "She was okay. And so was he. I don't think you need to worry so much about your dad. Maybe he's going to be all right."

Lucas pulls away. "And what if he's not? If something happens to Caitlyn because I wasn't looking out for her, it will be my fault. Not his." He pulls out his phone and calls someone from his contact list.

I sit down on the front porch step and watch him. His whole body is tense. Almost to the point of shaking. I wonder if I should have called him while we were at the cemetery.

"Hey, Cait. Where are you right now? . . . Really? Is Dad with you? Can I talk to him please?"

He turns away from me and starts walking back toward his car. I stand up to go back inside, my chest starting to hurt a little. At this point I kind of understand Starla. She realized there would never be enough room in Lucas's life for her.

But when I start to open the front door, Lucas calls out, "Wait."

I turn around. He puts his phone away. "I guess they're okay. I can't stay long, though. I thought Raine was going to take her to summer camp this morning."

"Why won't you just let your dad be a father, Lucas? You were there when he needed help, but now I think he's ready to step back up. You need to let him be the parent again."

"How do you know? How can I believe him?"

And I realize how similar Lucas and I are. We both have trouble trusting people who love us. Because we've been let down so many times before.

"Because you are a reasonable, kind, and trusting person. And I trust you," I say, the words heavy in my mouth. I must truly be crazy. Or fearless.

Lucas reaches out, cups my cheek in his hand. He doesn't say anything and for a moment I think I've said the wrong thing. But then he smiles. "I'm so glad." He pulls me close, bending his forehead to touch mine. "I trust you too."

I feel my eyes sting as I put both hands on his chest and push back. Gently. "You shouldn't," I say. "I might trust you, but I don't think I can trust myself."

"Natalie, when are you going to understand that you are not your grandmother?"

Of course he knows my worst fear. Even though I've never spoken it out loud. To anyone. "But what if I turn into her one day?"

He wipes away the tear leaking out of my right eye and it takes everything I have not to cave in to the enormous sob wanting to creep out of my chest. Lucas smiles shyly. "Your grandfather stood by her all those years. Why don't we just take it one day at a time and start with a dance?"

The Midsummer Night's Ball. I've forgotten all about tomorrow night's dance with everything else going on. I shake my head. "I don't think my parents are happy with me right now." And I don't mention how awkward and terrible it would be to see Mrs. Green and Starla again.

He nods. "Raine and I were willing to kidnap you if you still wanted to go. But if you'd rather just hang out—my house, your house, or at the Pirate House. Wherever. I'm fine with that, if you don't mind the company."

I hold his hands. Just being able to touch his skin, to breathe in the scent of him, is making me dizzy. "No, I wouldn't mind at all."

David's truck pulls up out front, sliding behind Lucas's Cherokee. "Should I move?" Lucas asks nervously. "I don't want to be taking his spot." I shake my head. "It's fine." But Mom is glaring at both of us when she gets out of the passenger side. David gets out too, glaring as well.

Colton gets out of the extended cab's backseat. At least he's not glaring at me.

Mom marches straight up to me. "Natalie Ann Roman, we've been all over this city looking for you. You need to say goodbye to this young man right now. You can talk to him later."

Lucas gives my hands a reassuring squeeze. "Call me," he whispers before heading back to his car. He easily maneuvers out from between David's and Dad's trucks.

I follow Mom inside, where Dad and Grandma are still arguing. David and Colton come in after us.

But Grandma takes one look at Colton and smirks. "Oh, look, David brought his cute little boyfriend home."

The living room falls deathly silent except for my gasp. "Grandma!"

Dad rolls his eyes. "That's enough, Mother. I think you need to go lie down."

Grandma looks around and realizes the damage she's done. Or maybe she doesn't. She winks at Colton. "Yes," she says slowly. "I'm not used to running the streets all night anymore. I could certainly use a nap."

Dad turns to Colton as Grandma retreats to her bedroom. "I'm so sorry. I have to apologize for her. She's not well." He holds his hand out. "Troy Roman. Pleased to finally meet you."

Colton blinks, and shakes my father's hand. "Colton Green."

"You knew?" David asks. "Did Grandma tell you?"

Dad shakes his head. "We've always known, David. You're our son. And if Colton's willing to accept the fact that you come from a batshit crazy family, and is willing to overlook that fact, then he's the best date you've ever brought home."

Mom tosses her purse down on the kitchen counter and grabs me in a fierce hug. "Do you know how worried we were?"

"I'm sorry," I whisper, still stunned that David is finally out to our parents, and it's all because of Grandma. And it wasn't a disaster.

But I suddenly realize how long it's been since I've had a shower, and the thought that I've been standing outside practically snuggling with Lucas while I smell like a homeless person horrifies me. "Ugh, I really need a shower."

Mom shakes her head. "First, we're going to talk about last night. I want to know why you didn't call us when Grandma wanted you to take her somewhere in the car."

"Or me," David says. "You know you should have woken me up. Mom and Dad came home this morning and I had no idea the two of you were missing." He's still giving me the evil eye, and yet I want to sigh with relief. He must not have told them about Mrs. Green and the theater.

David is the world's best brother. "I'm sorry," I say. "I just wanted to help Grandma."

Mom sighs just as Dad walks into the kitchen. "Now that they've got that car working, I guess we need to set some ground rules for Natalie using it." She gets a glass from the cabinet and fills it with water. "And how exactly did you get that car to run?"

I sit down at the bar. "Um, Caleb fixed it."

"Caleb?" Mom and Dad glance at each other. "What was he doing here?" Dad asks. "Did you invite him?"

I shake my head. "He came down with Trista and everyone to see the rehearsal. I think he came back just to talk with me."

"And he fixed the Jetta," Colton says, looking more than a little impressed.

"I told him it was over between us. I think he just needed some sort of closure. I'm pretty sure he's not coming back."

"Doesn't he have some sort of probation he violated by leaving Athens?" Dad asks. "Maybe we should call the authorities."

"Just leave him alone, Dad," I beg. "Please? He won't bother me again."

My parents exchange worried glances, but David doesn't say anything.

"Okay, so back to driving rules," Dad says. "We've been discussing how well you did with the play, and how we thought you might be ready to try a part-time job. And you will need one, to pay for insurance and gas."

I nod. "I can start looking next week," I say, trying to ignore my guilty conscience, which is screaming in my head that I DID NOT DO SO WELL WITH THE PLAY ARE YOU KIDDING, NATALIE ANN ROMAN?

And I don't think now is the right time to mention it, but I also want to go back to my doctor and see if he thinks I can decrease my medication again. Since I was never really hallucinating about ghosts in the theater.

David follows me up the stairs to my room. "Why the hell didn't you come get me last night? When Colton told me what had happened, I didn't want to believe him."

"I'm so sorry. I wanted to tell you . . ." But honestly, I think I was too scared last night that he wouldn't have sided with me either. "I didn't want you calling Mom and Dad and having them cancel their trip. They needed a break from here."

He scratches his scruffy hint of a beard. "Nat, I've been out all night looking for you. I'd come home just to see if you'd made it back yet and Mom and Dad surprised me."

I feel terrible, knowing he's been so worried all this time. I tell him about the trip to the beach and the cemetery. "You would have loved it," I say, wishing he'd been with us instead of Caleb. "She's crazy, but I still love her. And I know she loves us."

He leaves later in the afternoon with Colton to help with the final performance of the play. I'm sad that I'm missing it, but I'm also glad it's over. I don't want to see Raine and Starla ever again.

Colton pokes his head in the kitchen where I'm making a sandwich. "Lucas said to tell you hi. He would have come by if he could, but his dad was taking him and Caitlyn out for pancakes before the show."

"Good. I'm happy for them." And I am. Really. Breakfast for dinner is a huge step in his dad's rejoining the world of the living.

Colton frowns. "Listen. I don't know what my cousin and her friend did, but I want you to know that you deserve better. Fuck them. And that's all I'm going to say about it."

"Um, thanks."

"And if there's anything you want me to say to my aunt, I'll be happy to."

I sigh. I can't say anything without proof that Starla was tricking me. The fallen lighting rig? Probably an honest-to-goodness freak accident. The cold hands? Could have been someone hiding in the curtains. The footsteps in the rafters? Easily accessible from the ladder backstage. But there's no way I can link Starla to any of it.

Unless she confesses.

After the boys leave, I take a deep breath and find my parents sitting out on the back porch, holding hands. Maybe their shortened mini-vacation was useful after all. "Mom, the Midsummer Night's Ball is tomorrow night. We already have the tickets. And I'd like to go, just for a little while."

"Of course," Mom says. "Go have some fun. You've earned it."

No, I haven't. But I don't plan on having fun. I plan on putting an end to Starla's harassment.

CHAPTER 26

*If we shadows have offended,
Think but this, and all is mended,
That you have but slumber'd here
While these visions did appear.*

—*A Midsummer Night's Dream*, act 5

I decide not to tell Lucas I'm going to the ball anyway. I want to arrive on my own. Not like in an eighties teen movie grand gesture sort of way, but in a SNEAK-IN-WITHOUT-ANYONE-NOTICING sort of way. Instead of wearing the white chiffon dress Mom and I bought earlier this month, I find the black short dress I wore for homecoming last year, when Andria and I were goth homecoming ninjas.

"You're going to stand out if you aren't wearing white like everyone else," Grandma says, leaning against the doorframe of the kitchen. "But black does look good on you."

"Thanks," I say. I'm standing at the kitchen counter, taking my medicine.

She hands me the car keys. "I hope you find what you're looking for."

I take the keys from her, and we both stare at the pewter sand dollar on the key chain. "You did, right?" I ask her. "You found what you were looking for?"

My grandmother never smiles. But her face relaxes and for a moment she seems younger. "Yes. Yes, I did, Natalie."

I manage to get out the front door with Mom taking only two pictures of me dressed up. "Be careful," she says, kissing me on the forehead. "And have a good time."

I start the car, and Grandma's Beatles CD fills the interior. "In My Life." I turn the music down and drive off down the street toward the ball.

The dance is being held in the Fragrance Garden at Forsyth Park, where white lights and white rose garlands have been draped from each of the pavilions to give it a magical fairyland look. It's a steamy summer night and the air is heavy with the scent of roses.

A quartet is playing classical music right now, but Starla said a DJ would be playing dance music once it gets dark outside.

I don't see Lucas's truck in the parking lot. And I'm not sad. I'm here not for him, but to settle a score with Starla.

I show the doorman my ticket and he glances down at my black dress, but says nothing. I look nothing like the other girls drifting around in their white gowns. I no longer look like a fairy queen either. Maybe a vengeful dark fairy. The forgotten fairy godmother. I smile at the doorman and he looks at me nervously.

"Natalie! You came!" Raine rushes over to me, holding two cups of punch. "We didn't think you'd be here!" Her short white dress is strapless and she still hasn't put the blue streaks back into her black hair.

"I wanted to stop in just for a little while," I say. "Where is Starla?"

Raine hesitates and looks regretful. "I wish I'd known, Nat. About you."

"Have you been helping Starla trick me all along?"

"We were just having fun! You were the first one who mentioned the ghost, and we just wanted to see how far we could take it. I never knew you were schizophrenic. I'm so sorry."

"Did she tell you I had been at Winter Oaks?"

Raine shakes her head. "No. I didn't know. Honest. And I wish I had, because I never would have let you drink. I'm so ashamed, Nat."

But Starla acted like my best friend too before she turned on me. I still don't know if I can trust Raine or not. "Is she here yet?" I ask.

"I haven't seen her. Peter and I came together." Her eyes are shining brightly. Her goatee-sporting crush comes up behind her and she hands him a cup of punch. "Lucas didn't come with you?" she asks me.

I shake my head. "My decision to come was sort of last-minute."

"You should text him. I don't think he was planning to be here since you weren't coming," Raine says. "But he really needs to see you in that dress."

"I'd hate to drag him all the way out here when I'm not planning to stay long."

Raine stares at me. "Did you guys have a fight?"

Before I can answer, Mrs. Green comes up to us, with the mayor of the city. I almost abandon my plans for tonight. "Natalie, how are you feeling?" She doesn't say this like she really cares. She says it like she wants me to leave. How many lies has Starla told her about me?

"Much better, thank you." I smile at her and ignore the pain I feel. I used to like Mrs. Green. I thought she liked me, too. "I just couldn't miss tonight's ball." ACTING NORMAL, NOTHING TO SEE HERE.

Mrs. Green glares at me. "Yes, well. Have a good time, all of you. I don't suppose you've seen my nephew?"

Peter drains his cup of punch. "Colton was talking to the DJ a few minutes ago."

"Thank you. Stay out of trouble, children." Mrs. Green leads the mayor off toward the music.

Peter puts his hands around Raine's waist and kisses her neck. "Come here, child. I think you are the trouble that woman was warning me about."

She giggles and lets him lead her off to a rose-covered alcove.

Maizy is standing by the punchbowl with the twins. She is glaring at the string quartet, a dapper group of elderly gentlemen in tuxedos. "They could have hired us to play," she growls. She looks me up and down. "Nice dress."

"You play violin?" I ask.

"Yes."

"In a quartet?" I ask.

"A trio. Three girls. Our band is called Mourning Becomes Electra."

I stare at her. I haven't heard Maizy say more than two words to anyone all summer. And usually those two words are "fuck off." She scared Caitlyn and made the twins cry. "Cool," is all I can think of to say to her.

She's still glaring at the old men playing. I take a cup of punch and slink away from her, searching for Starla. And I wonder if Starla's prank might be one of the reasons that Maizy is such a bitch. Didn't Caitlyn say Starla told her aunt that Maizy was on drugs?

The night Starla locked me in the dressing room, I was terrified. When I realized she'd been deliberately trying to make me think I was crazy, I was furious.

Tonight, I am calm. And focused on revenge.

I find her standing just inside the garden gates, chatting with some of the people from Cast Three. Her white gown is long, edged in gold embroidery, and drapes over one shoulder like a Greek toga. She looks like a Greek goddess.

Her eyes grow wide as she sees me approaching her. I smile. I can tell it unnerves her.

Hunter, the dark-haired life guard from the pool, is standing with her. I almost don't recognize him in the tux, until he says, "Hey, it's the hot chick from the pool. Nice to see you didn't melt or explode or anything."

I shrug and give him a tiny smile. "You look wonderful, Starla."

"Score!" Hunter says, spotting a waiter with a plate of appetizers across the courtyard. "Be right back." He leaves Starla staring at me uncertainly.

"I thought you knew you're supposed to be wearing white."

I sigh, dramatically. "Don't you think white makes me look like a ghost?"

Starla glances around, not sure what I'm up to. I like that I've set her off balance. I want her to feel as unsettled as she's made me feel.

"Ever since I came to Savannah, I've had trouble figuring out what's real and what's illusion. I wanted to thank you for helping me to gain clarity."

She frowns, and looks a little confused. "Okay. You're welcome?"

"Starla! You made it!" Raine says, approaching us with Peter. "Where's Hunter?"

Peter is pulling on Raine's hand. "I thought we were going to dance."

"In a minute!" she says. "I wanted to make sure Natalie was okay."

"Never been better," I say, smiling.

Starla is glaring at me now, her arms crossed in front of her chest. "You don't look very stable to me, Nat. Maybe you should go sit down somewhere."

I shake my head. "I'm not afraid of you anymore." I think of all of our friends who've been hurt by Starla's lies and tricks. Maizy. Bethany. Lucas. Even Colton.

I could make sure everyone knows what she's been doing

behind all of our backs. Without proof though, I might end up sounding even crazier than I did two nights ago.

What if I scared everyone on purpose? I could claim that "voices" are telling me that Starla slept with Ferris. That Starla told Mrs. Green that Maizy was doing drugs. That she tried to get her cousin fired from the Pirate House.

Whether anyone believed in my "voices" or not, it would turn everyone against Starla. But is that what I really want?

I glance at Lucas, who's standing next to Ferris. He looks amazing in his tux. I want nothing more than to be dancing in his arms right now, but I need to finish this. Without ruining anyone else's night. I hope he understands. I don't want to scare him off.

Starla has shaken my ability to trust people. She knew my secret and used it to hurt me. The tears running down my cheeks aren't from acting. "Why?" I ask her. "Why would you trick me? Did you really hope I'd have a psychotic break and end up in the hospital or worse? Why would you lie about me?"

Starla starts crying too. "Because you swept in here and everyone loved you. You got the role I wanted. And you got Lucas."

"But you had Lucas," I say. "You gave him up." Lucas has moved away from Ferris and is now standing next to me. I take that as a sign of support.

Starla wipes her teary mascara-stained cheeks with her hands. "I went to Winter Oaks to tell him I was wrong. To tell him how sorry I was. And he told me it was better for both of us to move on. And then I saw you. And I saw him staring at you."

I can't help it. I look up at Lucas, shocked. He reaches out and takes my hand, gives it a squeeze.

Raine is still staring at Starla. "You really did lock her up and tell all those lies about her to your aunt? You're the crazy bitch here, Star. Not Natalie."

Starla rolls her eyes. "Whatever. I'm getting out of here."

She looks around, but Hunter, her date, has disappeared. With a heavy sigh and toss of her head she pushes past Raine and heads toward the garden's exit. She almost runs into Maizy and Mrs. Green.

Starla freezes, her face turning as pale as her dress.

Mrs. Green is frowning at her niece. "Miss Sanders tells me you have something to confess, Starla?"

"Oh hell," Starla grumbles.

"This could take a while," Raine whispers to me. "Obviously I suck at being a friend. Can you ever trust me again?"

As Mrs. Green stands at the entrance talking with Starla, her face grows more and more unhappy. Finally, Starla leaves in tears, and Mrs. Green comes over to us.

"Miss Roman, I believe I owe you a tremendous apology. Please forgive me. You are such a talented young lady. Please tell me you'll come back next summer and take part in our teen theater program again. I can promise that my niece will not be bothering you anymore."

"I'll definitely consider it," I say. Glancing over at Raine, I add, "If you'll be there next summer?"

Raine grins. "Wouldn't miss it."

Lucas puts his hand on my waist and leans close. "May I have this dance?" The elderly quartet has left and the DJ is setting up his equipment.

I look up at Lucas and everything in my chest explodes like fireworks. I nod and let him lead me to the center where couples are already gathering.

"Do you think it was wrong of me to talk to Starla like that?" I ask, trying to ignore the way his hands are settled on the curve of my waist. It takes all my strength not to just drag him off to a shady corner.

"You turned your weakness around, Nat. You stood up for yourself. And nothing you said was a lie. Apparently Starla has been hurting a lot of people. It was time everyone found out."

I lean my head against his shoulder and close my eyes just as the music starts. A little too fast for slow dancing, but Lucas doesn't make any move to pull away. I think I'm in love. I breathe in the scent of him, a mixture of coconut suntan lotion and cinnamon gum.

"Natalicious!"

I look up to see Colton and David headed toward us. "Are you guys ready to get out of here?" my brother asks. "I feel like Chinese food."

"Hungry?" Lucas asks. When I shrug, he smiles. "You can all ride with me."

I pull my keys out of my purse. I am smiling and giddy with happiness. "Let me drive."

Meet Natalie's friends in Robin Bridges's

DREAMING OF ANTIGONE

Available now in e-book and print format wherever books are sold!

"Heartfelt and emotional."
—Rebecca Phillips, author of *Faking Perfect*

"I can't ever be the blazing star that Iris was. I'm still just a cold, dark satellite orbiting a star that went super nova."

Andria's twin sister, Iris, had adoring friends, a cool boyfriend, a wicked car, and a shelf full of soccer trophies. She had everything, in fact—including a drug problem. Six months after Iris's death, Andria is trying to keep her grades, her friends, and her family from falling apart. But stargazing and books aren't enough to ward off her guilt that she—the freak with the scary illness and all-black wardrobe—is still here when Iris isn't. And then there's Alex Hammond. The boy Andria blames for Iris's death. The boy she's unwittingly started swapping lines of poetry and secrets with, even as she tries to keep hating him.

Heartwrenching, smart, and bold, *Dreaming of Antigone* is a story about the jagged pieces that lie beneath the surface of the most seemingly perfect life . . . and how they can fit together to make something wholly unexpected.

Connect with Us

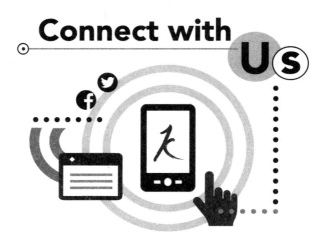

Visit us online at
KensingtonBooks.com
to read more from your favorite authors, see books
by series, view reading group guides, and more.

Join us on social media
for sneak peeks, chances to win books and prize packs,
and to share your thoughts with other readers.

**facebook.com/kensingtonpublishing
twitter.com/kensingtonbooks**

Tell us what you think!

To share your thoughts, submit a review,
or sign up for our eNewsletters, please visit:
KensingtonBooks.com/TellUs.